The Ancilian Forsvar

Book One:

Evocator
Crystallum

TOLV WALSTAD

Evocator Crystallum: The Ancilian Forsvar Book 1 © 2022 by Tolv Walstad

Copyright © 2022 by Tolv Walstad

Copyright © 2022 by Kriger and Vokter, LLC

All rights reserved.

ISBN: 978-1-958071-02-1

Published in the United States by Kriger and Vokter, LLC

Visit the Kriger and Vokter website to learn more

To my children, being a Hero is all about showing up when the going gets tough. Your gentle spirits and hearts have shown me what great Heroes you are. Thank you.

Find out what's *on the horizon* and
more about the author on the author's website

Prologus

Luke faced the Daemon as its leathery wings carried it down upon the castle wall before him. It was a bulky gargoyle-looking beast with red-hued eyes, wings splayed out to the side, a chiseled monstrous face with horns that jutted out from its head, bulky arms and legs, and a strong leathery tail that fell gently behind its body. It was a Volucer. Luke had already drawn blood with his ancile blades and knew that the window to see Lady Aurelia was closing.

The Daemon hissed, claws extended, leaping for Luke. He moved to the left, and his right ancile dashed upward. Claws flashed against the shielded front of the ancile, and the sharp iron cut deep into the Daemon's skin.

There wasn't another glance from Luke as he moved forward along the wall, rushing past the soldiers keeping watch. He wore his leather hauberk, with armored plates lining his arms to protect him from the blades. His short brown hair caught whatever breeze it could as he sprinted forward.

He glanced down to see a small Ancilian legion riding horseback toward the entrance of Arcem Regni. There he spotted his target, Lady Aurelia, at the front.

Luke couldn't help but catch a glimpse of the

Daemons outside the walls engaged in combat against the soldiers; the first line of defense before the Daemons could reach Arcem Regni, where they would face the full force of the Ancilian legions.

He found his way down the steps, sheathing his ancilia along his back, and moved through the crowded streets, reaching the front of the marching legion as the gates opened wide. He caught her eye just in time before they left.

Lady Aurelia reared her horse and moved toward him, followed by another soldier.

"Milady, there isn't time for this nonsense," the soldier with curly red hair spoke beside her as they came in range.

"It will only be a moment. I'll catch up with you soon." Aurelia said, waving him off.

"As you wish." He bowed his sharp chin and turned his horse toward the marching legion.

Luke stepped through the crowd and approached Aurelia. "Thought I wasn't going to have the chance to say goodbye."

Aurelia looked down at him, her dark-green eyes piercing his mind. Her glossy brown hair covered her forehead and was pulled back into a tight ponytail. Aurelia was one of the most influential people in the realm, and no matter how many times Luke gazed into her eyes, his heart skipped a beat.

"We're at war, and for the sake of the realm. You had to say goodbye?" She smiled, which made his smile appear.

"I would never miss the opportunity to say bye to you," Luke said and cleared his throat. "I wanted to make sure you were well equipped for your mission. Do you have the ancilia I made for you?"

She waved her hand at the sides of the horse to show the ancile blades sheathed behind the saddle. The shorter edge of the curved blade connected to the golden-shielded handle at the base, and the long, curved blade extended past the other side of the shield and was harnessed safely in its sheathed straps. "Wouldn't leave home without them."

He reached up and touched the small diamond he had attached to each shielded covering. "Had to make sure."

"Is that all you came to do?" she questioned.

"No. Make sure you come back to me," Luke said, grabbing her hands. "Life wouldn't mean anything if you weren't in it."

She gave a small laugh. "For the sake of the realm, I hope this isn't our last moment together."

"I should be going with you."

"You know as well as I do that you are needed here."

She squeezed his hands. "Once this is over, we'll hopefully have the chance to settle down and have a normal life."

"Valor!" A soldier called from the crowd, "You're needed on the wall; General wants all officers to report in."

Luke never turned to see the soldier calling him. He just stared into her dark-green eyes and soaked them in. "Be careful, and one last kiss before I send you off." Luke lifted his eyebrows, hoping for a kiss.

"That kiss will have to wait until I've safely returned. Duty to the realm and all." She pulled her hands back and turned her horse toward the gates. "Now get back to protecting the realm."

Her horse moved through the soldiers, making her way out the gates and to the front of the marching legion. The gates closed behind them.

He turned, rushing through the crowd to the wall. He told himself that he would have to stay alive long enough to get that kiss.

Luke approached from the west side of the wall to find himself the last officer to arrive, just in time to catch Marius Wilhelm's glance as he started to lay out the plan. The other officers stood upon the wall facing northeast toward the open fields. Daemons were scattered across the area, waiting to rush the walls.

"From here on out, we hold these walls until Lady Aurelia and her legion take down the Evocator and put an end to this madness," Marius said. "The Forsvar have sent warnings of small groups of Daemons approaching from each of the four corners of Arcem Regni. Our duty is to the realm and the citizens under our protection."

He continued, "We will each take a group of Ancilian soldiers and fortify the quarters of this wall. Under no circumstances are we to let a Daemon set foot past these walls, lest you find yourself dead and unable to swing your bloody weapon. Valor, you'll take the first section of the wall; Scorpio has the next section. Amata, you've got this section, and I'll take the last section. Questions?" No questions were raised. "Valor, a moment. The rest of you are dismissed."

Luke watched as the officers departed to their assigned areas. Beatrix Scorpio approached Luke; he saw that her white hair was layered from the back to the front to allow no hair to fall in front of her eyes. She stopped in front of him. Her ancile blades stood above her shoulders with sharply curved iron in their sheaths.

"Hope it was worth it," she said, her fierce blue eyes focused intently on his light-brown ones. "Glad you gave me the heads-up before you left your post and took off."

Luke kept staring her down. "Thanks for having my back."

She laughed and pushed past him. "Felt easier when you were out of the way; don't do it again."

"What does that mean?" he called after her, but she never looked back.

Marius was staring at Luke as he turned around; he had gray hair cropped short on the sides with short hair on top, in true legion fashion. "Sorry, sir."

"Valor, you left your post." Marius stepped toward him. "Lucky for you, Scorpio covered for you."

"Won't happen again, sir," Luke replied, standing at attention.

"May I ask why you left your post?"

"To see the Lady Aurelia and wish her success on her mission, sir," Luke responded.

Marius let the silence hang between them, then continued. "Heh. The protection of these citizens relies on each of us to make honorable decisions. Decisions that don't put anyone in harm's way. Even the Lady Aurelia lives and breathes those virtues." He paused. "How did she take you leaving your post?"

Luke thought before he spoke but knew that honesty was honorable among the Ancilians. "I didn't get that goodbye kiss, and she told me to get back to protecting the realm, sir."

Marius laughed. "Don't let her or the realm down then, or you'll never get that kiss. Now get to your post."

"Yes, sir." Luke started to walk toward his post and stopped. Something had been bothering him. "Why was I not assigned to go with her when there are plenty of other officers who can fortify these walls?"

"She didn't tell you?" Marius asked.

"Tell me what, exactly?"

"She requested for you to stay behind and protect the city."

Luke stood stunned. Aurelia had requested that he remain behind and took Felix with her. Of all the men in the realm, she had taken Felix with her. "Why would she take Felix instead of me?"

"Orders are orders. Take it up with her when she gets back. Now get to your post. They look like they are making their move." Marius looked upon the fields outside the city and found the Daemons stirring.

"Yes, sir." Luke saw the Daemons moving into packs and begin making their way forward toward the Ancilians, awaiting them at the walls.

He turned and headed toward his assigned section. He'd hold these walls for the next couple of hours, but once the initial incursion was over, he'd find a way to get Marius to let him ride after Lady Aurelia before she

got too far. Deep down, he knew something wasn't
right.

Chapter 1: Three Years Later

Lady Aurelia never returned from her mission, and nor did any of the Ancilians who had gone out with her. No matter how hard anyone looked, they never found her.

The Ancilian legions held the walls for nearly a day before a minor earthquake hit the realm and the number of Daemons began to diminish rapidly. The Ancilians made quick work of the last of the horde and waited hours for another assault, one that never came.

The Ancilians cheered, celebrating the success of Lady Aurelia and her legion, but she never returned. The cheering and celebrations became mourning, and search parties were sent to find her. To no avail.

The place of her last battle stood in ruins, with legion equipment and piles of bones scattered around, but none of the missing legion and Lady Aurelia.

Luke had volunteered to lead these search parties with the support of Lord Ursus, her father. They always ended the same way.

Days turned into weeks, weeks into months, and months into years. Luke never gave up on finding her and figuring out what happened.

During the spring, the rain fell steadily upon the stronghold of Arcem Regni. With the light of the sun beaming through the dark rain clouds, it was nearly half past noonday. Luke's steps toward the great gates brought water seeping from the ground to splash steadily against his boots.

A soldier yelled to open the gates as he approached. His birrus repelled most of the rain, but he still managed to get wet. At least during the springtime, it would keep him from freezing during these types of rainstorms.

The main entrance of the city was empty. The rainwater found its way through the stones and into the water canals. Soldiers stood guard near the gates, turning to face those who entered through these gates.

Luke saw Marius Wilhelm, general to the realm, stepping down the steps from the wall. "Valor, returning without your legion again?"

"They haven't arrived?" Luke turned his head. He saw no one out beyond the gates as they closed.

"They arrived a while ago, but without their commanding officer," Marius said, motioning for Luke to follow him under a tent.

Luke followed him to the tent and threw back his hood. His hair was sopping wet; he pressed his hand over it to remove the excess water. He knew that Marius wanted him to explain why his legion had shown up without him, but the old man already knew why. "There was an area that I felt we overlooked. Wanted to check it out."

"Find anything?" he asked.

"Nothing."

His voice came out stern and annoyed. "Why would any Ancilian overlook something when for the past three years, we've scoured the entire realm looking for her? This kind of insubordination was tolerable for the first year or two, but you need to let it go now."

The first year Luke would have lashed out. Marius's words would have gotten the better of him. Now he was just numb. "Understood. Won't happen again."

"See that it doesn't. We've all suffered enough; it's time for the realm to move on. You need to move on." He put his hand on Luke's shoulder. "Luke, the lord and lady have suffered enough—it is now time for you to let this become a part of your past and move forward with peace and hope for the future."

Luke looked up into Marius's green eyes as the rain beat heavily against the roof of the tent. "I've tried to let it go, move on from this heartache. I've lost a sense of my own identity and worth without her."

Marius squeezed Luke's shoulder. "You need to find meaningful purpose in life. I know that Lady Scorpio believes in you, and you should believe in her."

"Understood, sir." Luke acknowledged his words.

"Strength and honor," he responded, dropping his

hand.

"Strength and honor." Luke stood at attention and watched Marius head back toward the walls.

Luke threw his hood back up and briskly walked home through the rain.

Entering through the central castle gates, Luke turned within the courtyard toward the forge, where smoke rose steadily through the rainfall. He could hear the hammer hitting the anvil, and he threw back his hood as he passed under the stone walls and into the hearth of the forge.

"You're back!" called a young man working the bellows.

A young woman gazed up beside the anvil, slowing her hammer, and welcomed him back.

"How are things going?" Luke pulled off his birrus and tossed it upon a chair near the bellows to dry.

"These designs would be harder to follow without Cassia's help. Even though we've used these weapons for a decade or more, can't believe how hard it is to get them right," the young woman replied. Luke could see a pile of metal near her feet; they would have to be reforged at a later time.

"It takes time to learn how to craft the ancile, but once you've done it over and over, it does get easier. I promise," he replied.

They nodded and went back to work. Luke had started to take stock of everything in the forge when his mother stepped into the forge, removing her hood. Her long ash-brown hair peppered with gray flowed down to her shoulders and beyond. The delicate features on her face were covered slightly with scars.

"Luke, you need to let them do the work," she told him, shaking her head. "These forges continued while you were gone, and they won't stop running when we hand them over to someone else."

Luke set down a pair of ancile blades and looked up at her, seeing that her dark-brown eyes were intent on stopping him. "Understood, Mother. I wanted to see how things were coming along."

"You are trying to distract yourself from your newfound duties to the realm." She placed her hand over his. "Put it down."

Luke had to force himself from checking the next set of ancilia. Knowing she was right about the situation wouldn't make it easier to let it go. He *was* trying to distract himself from his duties.

"What would you have me do with my time?" he asked.

"Let's speak of these things at home. Do you require any assistance from us?" she asked, turning toward the young man and woman.

They replied with a no and thanked her for all she had instructed them. Then she headed toward the entrance, waving at Luke to follow.

Luke grabbed his birrus, threw it over his head, and followed his mother around the corner to their home.

Once inside, he tossed it aside again and jumped right into the discussion. "I understand that they expected this from me years ago, but it was different back then."

His mother lowered her hood and started to pour herself a glass of water. She offered one to him. He declined.

"The apprentices need to take over the forge, and that won't happen if you keep interfering with their work," his mother replied.

"Their work? Father started and worked the forge day and night for this realm, and look where it got him."

"Don't speak ill of your father. May he rest in peace, without you dragging him into this." She sat down at the table and waved for him to sit with her.

Luke yanked the chair out and roughly sat down. "Apologies, Mother, but do you think it wise for us to hand over the forge?"

She sipped at her water, nonresponsive to his

question.

"Even with my responsibilities changing, I'd like to continue to further the work that Father and you started with the ancile. Every time I craft one, I feel the design sifting ever so slightly, one more step toward perfection."

"Don't forget who worked with your father to make the first ancile," she said.

"I know." He stood up and walked over to a wooden closet set against the wall and opened its doors. Inside, hanging on wooden pegs, sat a pair of ancile blades with armor set between them. "Every time I look at these, I am amazed at what he created. Then I realize that no matter how hard we try to find the materials he used, they just don't exist."

The ancile blades were different from those designed for the Ancilians. They were crafted with material not found in the realm. Etched into the armor was an image of a phoenix rising from the ashes, marking a new beginning. The ancile blade was gripped by a side handle about two-thirds of the way down the blade. The blade was slightly in front of the fist and extended the full length of a person's arm, ending by the shoulders. Attached above and below the handle were small shields, providing extra protection to the wearer.

The plated armor was dented and scarred from the war, and along the top of the armor were two significant puncture marks beside the shoulder pads. The sleeves were covered with sharp, jagged edges.

The material never dulled even through the constant combat his father had been in; Luke's mother had told him about the blades, but it overwhelmed him. Luke closed the closet and placed his head on the wooden doors.

"He wanted you to have that when you came of age." His mother's voice rose behind him.

Luke never wanted to touch them again. The one time he had tried was enough for him. Never again. "These belong where they are, shut behind wooden doors." He turned toward his mother. "Marius told me that I needed to leave it behind me and move on. That it would be best for the realm."

"The past doesn't define who we are, but it does define who we are destined to become. Your father knew that better than anyone. If he were asked if he'd change anything about his past, he'd be the first to tell you no. It never held him back, and you shouldn't let it get its hold on you." She had gradually crossed the room and hugged him.

Luke was taller than his mother; avoiding the spikes in her shoulders, he returned the hug before stepping away. "Did you find yourself losing who you were after he was gone?"

"Never. Though I grieve without him, it never stops me from doing what I have to do." She made her way back to the table and took a sip of water.

"I'm trying to not let it stop me." He looked up, feeling the exhaustion set in. He was ready to lie down, and it had only begun to get dark.

There came a knock on the door.

Luke composed himself and opened the door. A soldier stood outside in the rain.

"Yes?"

"Sir, Lady Ursus wishes to speak with you," the soldier told him.

"I'll be right there," he told the soldier. He quickly removed his ancile blades from his back and dropped them near the closet. Then he grabbed his birrus while looking at his mother. "Duty calls."

Chapter 2: Audience with Regium

Luke made his way up the stone steps to the courtyard outside the throne room halls. The rain fell steadily, pelting the stonework, and splashed into the fountain in front of the main doors. In the center of the fountain stood a statue of Aurelia. It had been erected in the last year, when they had given up hope of finding her.

She stood facing forward wearing the Ancilian armor, hair falling perfectly around her face down to her shoulders. Her cloak billowed out behind her while her left foot pressed down upon a Daemon, its wings unfurled to the sides. In her right hand, she held the infamous ancile blade.

The rain made her look menacing. Luke knew that underneath her fierceness was the kindhearted girl he had fallen in love with. The statue was a reminder of a past that no longer was.

He moved past the statue and found the guards opening the iron doors for him. He proceeded through the throne room and down an adjacent hall, with torches lighting the way. He saluted the soldiers as he passed them, and they acknowledged him in turn.

Turning the corner, he slowed his approach. Down the hall he spotted Lady Scorpio, wearing a white gown that flowed down to her ankles. Except for her left shoulder, her exposed arms were draped with the cloth falling down over them. A golden weaved belt was wrapped about her waist, and her arms were clasped with gold jewelry. The sandals upon her feet, with leather straps wound up her ankles, made her stand an inch taller.

She glanced his way, and he corrected his approach and picked up the pace. He walked until he stood next to her and faced the door with her.

"Milady Scorpio," Luke said.

"Lord Valor," she replied.

"Looking beautiful as ever," he said, admiring her clothing.

"My thanks, and you're looking—ruggedly handsome tonight." She looked him up and down. "Am I to presume that you just arrived home?"

"Yes," he said, reaching to touch the scruff on his face. He hadn't had time to clean himself up, and he had been drenched in the rain. "Didn't think we had to dress up to meet with the lord and lady of the realm."

"Not particularly, but it never hurts to make an impression," she responded.

As he started pulling off his birrus, the collected drops of water flew around him. "Not my fault it's raining hard out there."

"I find it endearing," she said.

"Only you would," he replied.

She sighed. "Wish you would have taken me with you on your last mission. I am tired of being confined to these walls."

"We don't have a choice, and with how things are going, we may not get the chance to leave these walls for a while." His arms waved at the stones surrounding them.

"Don't say that. Even the thought of it is horrifying." She sighed. "Oh how quickly things have changed."

Luke knew exactly what she was talking about. The last three years had changed everything, and they were caught up in the heart of it. He reached out and grabbed her hand. "We're going to make the best of it, and I'm grateful to be by your side."

She squeezed his hand back. "As am I."

Footsteps approached the door, and the iron door opened. The soldier waved them inside, taking Luke's birrus, and they walked hand in hand into the room.

A blazing fire burned on the far corner of the room, and torches gave their dancing light. Opposite to the fire was a bed, hefted off the ground by wooden beams, and on the bed was Lord Ursus lying on his back, his face pale.

Lady Ursus sat beside her husband and held his hand as they entered. She waved them to his bedside and told the soldier to wait outside.

"Thank you for coming on such short notice," she told them. "No matter what care we give him, his condition never changes. It keeps on getting worse."

Lord Ursus pushed himself up in his bed against his wife's complaints. "Now isn't the time to show complete and utter weakness."

She helped him sit fully up in bed. "If you insist."

"Lord Valor and Lady Scorpio," Lord Ursus spoke in a low, weary voice, "with the last of the life in me...I want to be part of the ceremony, and with how fast I am deteriorating, that may be sooner than we had originally anticipated."

Luke felt his heart quicken. He wasn't ready for all of this. They had possibly another year or two before the official coronation from their previous discussions. "Lord Ursus..." he began, stopping when he saw Lord Ursus's hand raise to silence him. He glanced over at Beatrix and could see that her eyes were wide.

"Young Lord Valor, let me finish." He continued, "However your wishes may be, the realm needs strong leadership. With the guidance of my wife and others, you two shall find your way in leading the realm together. These circumstances have placed us in a situation of our own doing. Without Aurelia"—he paused, choking on her name—"the order of succession has been passed to our adopted daughter, Beatrix.

"Luck would have it that the two of you care for one another and have been lifelong friends." He continued, "I know that when we promised not to interfere in your courtship, and that it wasn't our place, given the circumstances…However, do either of you have any concerns about why we shouldn't move forward with the coronation?"

Beatrix went first. "Though I'd prefer more time, there are no concerns."

Luke was amazed that Beatrix hadn't hesitated at all. Over the last couple of years, he had been able to confide more in Beatrix. Though they grew up together and had become lifelong friends, his heart had belonged to another. But with Aurelia's passing years ago, he had been given another chance at love and found himself falling more for Beatrix over the last year. He remembered what Marius had told him about moving on. Now was an excellent chance to step forward. "Would always love to have more time," he said, squeezing Beatrix's hand. "No concerns."

She squeezed his hand back.

Lord Ursus smiled and then choked down a cough. "Then may we proceed with the coronation before I head to my grave?"

Luke and Beatrix looked at each other and nodded

anxiously.

Lord Ursus fell into a coughing fit before he could respond. Lady Ursus helped him drink a glass of water and lie back down.

"Give me a moment. I will fill you in on the rest of the details," Lady Ursus said as she soothed her husband's forehead with a damp cloth.

Once he was settled, she waved them away from the bed toward the fire. "Stubborn fool doesn't know how weak he truly is. Always pushes himself."

"Did the physicians ever figure out how father's health rapidly declined?" Beatrix asked, keeping her voice low.

"They aren't sure how it happened, but they believe that he was infected. They are unsure of the source, though," Lady Ursus said, her hands pressed tightly together. "I don't know how he was infected without others falling to the same illness and how I escaped his same fate."

Luke wanted to say something but was unsure how to start discussing how the lord of the realm was infected in the first place. "I'm sorry," he said finally.

"It isn't your fault. At first we thought it was a broken heart from losing Aurelia. Though many of us suffered during her loss, he got worse and worse. Slowly his body just wasn't the same."

"Mother." Beatrix stepped toward her, giving her a hug.

She hugged her and quickly withdrew. "My dear child. Don't let him see us this way. For the sake of the realm, he needs to see strength without weakness."

Beatrix glanced back at her father upon his bed, resting. "I understand. Strength and honor."

"Which brings me to the next topic of our conversation. General Wilhelm has been receiving warnings from the Forsvar about another invasion from the Daemons, which is also why we should hasten the coronation, to show strength and unity in the realm. We've had nearly three years of peace, but that may be coming to an end."

She continued, "Luke—Lord Valor, please have General Wilhelm fill you in on the details in the morning, and begin preparations of the legions in case another war is to befall the realm."

Luke nodded.

"Lady Scorpio, please sit with me to discuss our continued investigation into your father's condition and the details of the coronation. Lord Valor, you are dismissed."

Luke lifted Beatrix's hand and kissed it. "Milady." As he headed for the door, he glanced back and watched Beatrix and Lady Ursus take a seat near the fire. Luke hadn't decided if he was ready for the life of being lord of the realm. He had grown up in the legions, and it was going to be very different than what he was used to. The soldier handed him his birrus as he passed, and he continued down the hall, through the throne room and into the courtyard beyond. The rain had been relentless. The sun had started to dip toward the western mountains, causing the light to fade entirely from behind the clouded sky.

He put his birrus back on, stepping out into the rain, past the statue of Aurelia. He had a distinct feeling that someone was watching him.

Chapter 3: Shadows of the Past

Luke closed and bolted the door behind him, finding his mother huddled over the table, going through a box.

"Mother, going through your old things?" Luke asked as he walked through the door, pulled off his birrus in a rush, and tossed it over a chair.

She glanced up at him and found his hands signing, "*Keep talking—someone is following me.*"

Luke had learned how to sign during his time in the legion. Since the realm had started working with the Forsvar, learning to communicate with signs had become a key element to working with them.

"Trying to find something," she said. Her hands then began to sign back. "*Who is following you?*"

"*Couldn't see them out in the rain,*" he signed. He moved over and picked up his ancilia, strapping them to his back. Then he continued signing. "*Walked around for a bit to see if I was imagining things. Definitely felt like someone was watching me, but I saw nothing.*"

His mother moved over and lifted the hood of a chest near her bed. She lifted her own ancilia, then laid them on the bed. "*Is there only one?*" she signed.

"*I don't know,*" he signed, then let his hands fall to

his side.

"How was your visit to Lord Ursus?" she asked.

"They want to move up the coronation date," Luke said. "Did you find what you were looking for?"

"I see that you are not wanting to talk about it, but no, I didn't find what I was looking for."

Luke lifted his hands and signed, *"His wife believes that he's been infected, but they don't know how it was only him."*

"Infected?" she signed back.

"Yes. I wanted to know more but was occupied with the coronation being moved up," he responded in sign.

"How is Beatrix doing with all of this?" she asked.

"Good. I assume," he responded, walking toward the door. Luke listened for any sound other than the wind and rain. Nothing.

"When was the last time you spent time alone with her?" His mother moved back toward the table, feeling that the danger was evidently over. "I do remember the way that your father courted me; I might be able to provide some help."

"I'll pass." He moved to the table. "Though you're right. I need to find time for us to get away and talk about this whole situation. It's all happening so fast, and I don't even have time to process what's going on."

"That's how it was for your father and me," his

mother interjected.

"Your courtship will always be very different than mine. Not sure it's fair to compare the two."

"Your father. Nero, I remember it as vividly as if it were yesterday." She stared off into the distance. "The way he commanded the room whenever he entered. Everyone looked at him in their darkest hour, and I was in love. Oh, how I wish he were still with us."

"Not sure what to say anymore. One second we're talking about my situation and the next you're off dreaming about him again."

She lowered her eyes and glanced over at him. "You look just like him, except he was exceptionally more handsome."

"Not helping." Luke smiled and leaned his head down. "What would he do in my situation?"

"Sweep the woman off her feet!" she exclaimed, throwing a small cloth at him from the box.

"Yeah, you've lost it." Luke turned around. He went to the door and checked for sounds again, then signed to his mother that there was nothing but rain.

"Beatrix deserves your full attention; I've seen the way you've been distracted. All of us have."

Luke had been distracted. Marius was right about him not letting go of his past and moving on. "I'm trying," he said. "Even Marius told me to move on and not hold on to the past. Been trying to shake the feeling that something is off about the whole thing, even after these three long years. I have this feeling in my gut— can't shake it."

"Your father followed his gut." She stopped ruffling through the box. "What's your gut telling you?"

"That she's out there somewhere."

"She may be, but after all this time, things have changed. You've changed. Things wouldn't be the same if she showed up now. They would be different."

Luke felt his heart pounding. Everything had changed. His friendship with Beatrix had transformed into something more. It had been three years, and he still thought that Lady Aurelia was out there. He could remember the feeling of waiting for her to return, awaiting that kiss that never came, to see her smiling face once more.

He slammed his fist on the table. "My thoughts keep betraying me. How do I forget about her and move on? Everyone else has."

"The realm mourned the loss of their lady. Lord and Lady Ursus have been heartbroken ever since. To say otherwise is you being ignorant of their feelings."

"Ignor…" He stopped himself, took a deep breath, and tried to compose himself. "It's hard for me to move on, and it feels that others have been able to let go."

"No one truly lets go. They grieve in different ways; everyone has to find some way to cope with loss. Not a night goes by that I don't wish I could have saved your father, but I cope with it very differently than you do."

"I'm sorry. I know that bringing this up always reminds you of losing Father." Luke went over to comfort his mother, putting his arm around her. "I'm sorry."

"Not a day goes by that I don't grieve his loss, but when I look at you, I see that we were given a second chance. I hate seeing you give up on the dream your father had for you." She turned toward him, placing her hand on his shoulder. "He would be proud of the man you are today and would tell you that he loves you."

Luke looked down at the ground, barely holding tears back. Growing up without his father had been tough. Seeing him lying in a bed being tortured had been hard for him to see. He remembered sitting beside his bed, talking of his many adventures with his mother, but when the night came, he would fight to stay awake, arguing with his mother about where his father was and that they would to get him out. Eventually, he'd fall asleep, and it began all over again, night after night until it was over.

He had been young enough to remember a few details of those nights, but he had tucked most of those memories away, not wanting to relive them. Tonight, he felt that maybe if he started to face those critical moments from his past, he would finally be able to let go.

"One of these days, I want to know what happened to him," Luke said, looking at his mother.

She looked into his eyes and then turned away. "It's complicated."

"From what I understand about the Forsvar, it's essentially living between two worlds." Luke tried to remember the word they called the other place but couldn't remember. "They live in this one but walk in the other, right?"

"I promised him that I would tell you all about it." She shook her head. "You aren't ready."

Luke was taken back. "What, why?"

"There is already so much happening in your life; this would only add to the complexity. I'm sorry, but I won't."

Luke wanted to push the discussion; he was ready to face his past. But he could see that his mother wasn't willing. He shouldn't push her, but he found himself biting his tongue. "When will you be ready?"

"It isn't about when I am ready." She turned toward him, her face serene. "You aren't."

The pain struck. He shouldn't have said anything.

He turned and lifted a glass, filling it with water and drinking it down. He hoped that it would dislodge the lump in his throat and alleviate the sting but the only way was to know why.

"How am I not ready?" Luke turned to face his mother. "When will I…?"

Three loud thuds slammed against their door, pushing the door inward. The force against the door was strong enough to break it down.

Luke rushed to the door and threw his body against it. His mother raced across the room, her ancilia in her hands. There was a loud thud against the ground outside.

She stepped toward the door and signed. "*Open it on the count of three.*"

Her fingers counted, one by one. Luke threw the bolt and placed his hands behind his back onto the handles of his ancilia.

Three. Luke pulled the door open, turning with his mother flanking on the side. Outside, the wind howled, and the rain slammed against the city's stones. There on the ground was something wrapped in heavy cloth.

When they found no one to be about, Luke retrieved the cloth and brought it inside. He set it on the table and began unwrapping it.

Inside was a broken golden ancile, a small diamond

attached to the shield covering, and a piece of parchment paper. He reached down, clearing away the dirt surrounding the diamond. His eyes caught a glimpse of a shadow near the door. He turned, but it was gone.

Then he looked back at his mother, knowing what this was. "She's alive."

Chapter 4: Aurelia's Ancile

She looked back at him and said, "How do you know that it is hers?"

"The diamond attached to the shield. Look." He reached down, pointing to the diamond found under the dirt. "The gold plating, the diamond. I know this is hers—it's the one I made for her."

He lifted the parchment and read it aloud. "Rubrum Castellum."

"The ruins?" his mother asked. "From previous accounts, they found nothing there."

"Then why would this show up? There has to be something we overlooked." Luke reached for his birrus. "I need to know."

"We should first speak with Marius about this, and it's already dark. Let it be for the night."

"They need to know that their daughter may still be alive; this may give them the hope they've been looking for." Luke pointed toward the broken ancile on the table. "This is the first clue we've had in years. We can't wait another moment."

Luke reached forward, finding his mother's outstretched arm stopping him. "We don't even know how this got here or who left it. You're rushing ahead without thinking it all the way through."

Luke stepped back. He didn't care that he wasn't thinking straight. For the last three years, they had searched and found nothing. Now a piece of a missing puzzle had arrived, and he wasn't going to wait. He pushed past his mother, grabbing the ancile off the table, and turned for the door.

He stopped instantly as his eyes drifted upon the shadowy figure standing at the door. It hovered cloaked in a brown robe, a hood draped over its face and darkness filling the void underneath. It hovered side to side without legs. Then its robed arm lifted toward him, but its hands were gone.

Luke dropped the ancile to the floor, reaching for his own blade, and the figure disappeared.

It had all happened so quickly that his mother's arms were still outstretched to keep him from sprinting out the door. "Stop!"

"Did you see that?" he asked calmly. His hand was still on his ancile, but he dropped his hand to the side when he saw nothing in front of him.

She peered past him. "See what?"

"The shade or whatever it was. Right near the door." He pointed. "It's gone now, but it was right there."

"There isn't anything there now." She moved past him and picked up the ancile. "Now I see it." She barely moved upward and then dropped the broken ancile back to the floor. "It's cursed."

"What's cursed?"

"The blade, that shade you saw. It's following that." She pointed to the broken ancile on the floor as she moved to the counter and wiped her hands on a cloth. Then she signed to him, *"I don't know if it can hear us. That thing needs to be destroyed."*

He signed back to her. *"We can't just destroy it—not yet. It's the only thing we have that shows Aurelia is still alive. Once I've talked with the Lord and Lady Ursus, we'll destroy it. I have to show them the proof."*

She hesitated and then signed back, *"Once you have spoken with them, bring it to the forge, and we'll destroy it."* She reached, tossed him the worn out cloth, and signed again, *"Wrap it in the cloth."*

He nodded to her, reached down to pick up Aurelia's ancile with the cloth. The shade didn't reappear.

"Do you see it?" she asked.

"No," he replied.

"You know what you must do," she told him.

"I know." Luke tightened his grip on the cloth-wrapped ancile and picked up the parchment paper from the table, then turned toward the door, heading out into the moonlit rainfall.

The soldier knocked on the door to Lord and Lady Ursus's chamber. "Lord Valor is here to speak with you."

"Tell them it is urgent," Luke whispered to the soldier.

"He says he has urgent business that he wishes to discuss with you," the soldier spoke through the door.

Lady Ursus opened the door, waving him in. "This had better be worth it."

The soldier stopped him. "Please leave your ancilia with me."

Luke removed the ancilia from his back and handed them to the soldier. He could see Lord Ursus lying on the bed, snoring.

Lady Ursus walked over to the fireplace and urged him to sit. "What business do you have at this hour?"

"I found this at my door." He unfurled the cloth surrounding the ancile.

"A broken weapon?" She rolled her eyes, standing up. "You got me out of bed for this nonsense? Soldier."

The soldier started toward them.

"This was hers," he said quickly.

She lifted her hand, and the soldier stopped. "What do you mean?"

Luke showed her the note and told her that he had crafted the ancile before Lady Aurelia left on her last mission. She had these exact ones with her.

"Rubrum Castellum is in ruins. Has been since the last war. Although if I remember correctly, it was where Aurelia went," she said, falling back in her chair. "What does this mean?"

"It means that she may be alive," Luke said.

"Stop it! My heart cannot take the false hope any longer, and if Cyrus were to hear you speaking, it would kill him."

"I may be old, but I am not deaf." Cyrus Ursus had thrown back the covers and sat up in his bed. "My daughter is alive?" He looked at Luke with eyes full of longing.

Luke stood up. "We don't know that for sure, but this is the closest thing we've found since she went missing."

Lady Ursus leaped off the chair and headed toward her husband. "We don't know anything for sure. It is all speculation at this point, and you need your rest."

"I thought that I could go to my grave knowing that Aurelia was waiting on the other side for me. That I would once again hold my little girl." Cyrus lowered his head. "It gave me hope knowing she was there, and I wouldn't be alone. But now, now you bring this…this thing into my chambers and tell me that my daughter may be out there alive and alone?"

Luke could feel the same hope he had been looking

for seep into his heart. Where had she been all this time, and was she alone, waiting for them to find her?

"Don't you see what you've done." Lady Ursus looked at him, fire in her eyes. "This is all just speculation. We'll send the soldiers to check out Rubrum Castellum in the morning. For now, we all need our rest."

She turned to her husband and tried to help him lay back down. He stayed firmly upright. "I thought she was dead," he told her. "I can't die knowing she is out there alone."

"Look at what you've done!" she yelled at Luke. "Soldier, get Marius."

The soldier saluted and quickly left to get Marius.

"I had to show you before..." He stopped himself. Explaining that the ancile was cursed would only complicate the situation further.

Lady Ursus was looking at him for an answer.

"...before I headed to the ruins myself," he finished.

"Absolutely not! With the coronation happening in a few weeks' time, you need to be here," Lady Ursus commanded, lifting a damp rag to her husband's head.

Luke had to stop himself from saying something he would regret. He held his tongue, wanting to tell them that there was nothing more important than finding Aurelia, and keeping him held up in the city when he had just gotten the only clue to finding her wasn't going to happen.

The soldier entered the chamber and announced that Marius was here.

Marius Wilhelm walked into the chamber. He carried a single ancile blade on his back. His eyes met Luke's as he entered, and he immediately knew there was trouble.

Lady Ursus quickly caught Marius up on the situation, detailing what Luke had told them.

"The soldiers have checked Rubrum Castellum multiple times. It was the key point of our investigation into the disappearance of Lady Aurelia," Marius said, his eyes drifting back and forth between Luke and Lady Ursus. "Lord Valor should have brought this to me first."

Luke lowered his head. How much should he share with Marius on the cursed ancile? Very little at the moment, he figured. "When this arrived at my doorstep, I couldn't wait another moment, knowing she is out there."

"Heh. You only thought of yourself in this situation. You barged in on the lord and lady of the realm to bring them false hope that their daughter may be alive when we have covered the entire realm in our investigation," Marius said. "But you find this broken blade and want to tell the entire realm that Aurelia is alive!"

Marius continued angrily, "Earlier you arrived without your legion, stating that you wished to investigate something you felt we had overlooked. When are you going to stop acting for yourself and act like a lord of the realm?"

Luke clenched his fists, his hands tightening around the cloth. "I never chose to be lord of the realm."

"That's what you are to become, so start acting like it. Aurelia gave her life for the realm, and here you are dragging her name through the mud with your false hope."

Luke's fists loosened and tightened. He wanted to punch Marius in the face. It would have been better if he hadn't said anything to anyone and had just gone to Rubrum Castellum himself. "I stepped out of line. I let my feelings get the best of me."

Marius waved his hand in dismissal of his words. "Show me the broken ancile."

Luke unrolled the cloth.

"You made this for her, and she left with it that day?" Marius asked, reaching for it.

Luke pulled back and wrapped the cloth around it again, not wanting Marius to touch the cursed ancile.

"What are you hiding?" Marius lifted his eyebrows.

"Nothing." Luke handed the parchment to Marius,

avoiding further questions.

"Anyone could have written this, and having only the broken pieces of a weapon is not proof enough for an investigation." Marius handed the parchment back.

"I'm going," Luke insisted. "Tomorrow morning, I am going to Rubrum Castellum and seeing it through myself."

Marius glanced at Lady Ursus, who was shaking her head. "We'll send a small legion out in the morning to investigate the ruins. However, Lady Ursus has made her wishes known, and you won't be joining."

"There is nothing stopping me from leaving and doing this on my own," Luke said, stuffing the wrapped cloth into the ancilia straps along his back. "I'll take my leave now. Lord and Lady Ursus, my apologies."

He stepped forward, and Marius pushed him back. "One moment, please." Marius glanced over to Lady Ursus. "He's stubborn like his father and won't take no for an answer."

"Place him under house arrest until the investigation has completed." She waved her hand toward Marius, and the soldier behind him moved forward.

Luke stepped back from them as they approached.

"Come with us," Marius ordered. "As a citizen of the realm, you are hereby placed under house arrest until further notice."

Luke moved to the side and put a chair between him and Marius. He shoved the chair toward Marius and then sprinted for the door. Luke shoved the soldier out of his way as Marius threw the chair aside and slammed his boot into his back.

Luke fell to the floor and felt the weight fall upon him. His arms were brought behind his back, and he was pulled up to his knees. Marius gripped his wrists and lifted him off the ground.

He glanced up toward the door to see Beatrix staring at the scene. He could see the astonishment in her eyes as they walked past her and down the hallway.

Shame washed over Luke as he lowered his head and stopped resisting.

Chapter 5: The Evocator's Shade

Marius shoved Luke into a room down the hall and stationed soldiers outside the door. Luke opened the door once and found four soldiers staring back at him. They slammed the door shut, and he was alone.

Luke paced around the room, anger washing over him. Why was Marius upset with him for bringing the lord and lady a clue about their daughter? He wanted to give them hope that she was out there, the hope he had felt when seeing it for the first time, and now he was under house arrest.

He slammed his fist down upon the table and felt some of his anger dissipating. What he didn't understand was why. Why couldn't he go with the legion to investigate the clue they received? He knew they wouldn't be as thorough as he would. He wouldn't leave until he had completed a full detailed investigation. Every rock, nook, and cranny would be searched until he figured out what happened.

He slammed his fist again. Marius, the look he had given him, the way he lectured him. It was irritating. No matter what he did, he'd get that look of disappointment. Marius had been a longtime family friend and had been there at his father's passing, comforting his mother and whispering about things he couldn't remember.

Why wouldn't his mother share the details of his father's passing with him? Why did she think he wasn't ready to know?

Luke kicked a chair to the side, and a soldier opened the door giving him a menacing look. He raised his hands in apology and picked up the chair.

What had she meant about adding complexity to Luke's life? What complexity? Losing his father at a young age? Mysteries of his passing? Aurelia going missing for the last three years? Falling in love with her adopted sister Beatrix? Going to be crowned lord of the realm…?

Marius was right. He wasn't acting like someone who was about to be crowned lord of the realm, to reign beside Beatrix. She was more capable than he was, and he wasn't even focusing on how or what his part would be.

Luke found his way to a bench on the wall and sat down, dropping his face into his hands.

Giving up the forge his father had created for the realm, pushing his mother for knowledge, disregarding her feelings when he needed to focus elsewhere. Beatrix being forced into becoming lady of the realm. Had he really thought about how it would affect her? Marius was right. He had only been thinking about himself.

For the past three years, he had pursued the long-lost Aurelia, putting all his focus into finding her. The neglected forge and his mother, Cassia, had to perform the duties without his assistance. It had been a duty that she and her husband did together. Luke pulled at his hair. She was alone, and maybe she didn't even have the answers she wanted but she kept pushing forward through the grief and pain.

Even his duties to the legion were awful. He was neglecting training routines for additional searches that were unsanctioned by Marius. Now it made sense why he had gone off on Luke like he did. He was tired of his outbursts, cries for attention, the needless cause of pain and anguish to the Ursus family.

Still, Luke felt like his questions were going unanswered. He wasn't ready to hear the truth about his father, though his mother said that she promised his father that he would tell him. Not prepared, she said. Luke pushed off the bench, moving to the table, gripping the edges.

When would he be ready? That is what he should have asked. What did he need to do to prove that he could get the answers he wanted?

He lifted the table off the ground but stopped himself before flipping it. Being in the room wouldn't get him the answers he wanted, and trying to figure it out himself was driving him mad.

Sitting upon the bench, he realized that he had let them all down. His father, for not being strong or big enough to help. Aurelia, for letting her go alone and not being there. His mother, for letting her grieve and suffer alone. His duties to the realm. To Marius and Beatrix, a friend that had become much more over the last three years. He should have paid more attention to the things around him than the past.

Luke leaned back against the wall and felt the broken ancile against him. He leaned forward and pulled it out from the straps on his back. Why did this thing have to show up now, when everything was already a mess?

Unwrapping the cloth, he stared down at the broken ancile once more. Luke knew that he should have destroyed it when he had the chance earlier, but it had hit the depths of his broken heart, and he had to know.

Letting out a sigh of anguish, he chucked the cloth and broken ancile across the room. They scattered and slammed against the stone wall. He felt foolish for everything he had done in the last hour.

The look on Beatrix's face when he walked by…he bet they were filling her in on all the things he had said and done. What would she think of him after this, dragging her sister, his old love, back into their lives?

He should have just let it go. Where had Aurelia's ancile been all these years? His eyes lifted to the broken piece on the floor, and he slowly moved toward it.

Maybe he could let it go after a few more questions.

He decided to pick up the broken ancile with his bare hands, knowing all the while that he should pick the up with the cloth.

The shade appeared in the corner of the room, hovering side to side in its brown hooded cloak.

"I guess you're stuck with this." Luke moved to the side, and the shade followed. "Why are you following it?"

Luke felt odd talking to the shade, but it was better than speaking to himself at the moment.

He moved toward the bench and sat back down, watching the shade follow him at a distance.

"What are you?" he asked.

The shade slowed and stopped.

Luke stared at the shade and saw the emptiness underneath.

"Guess I was hoping you'd have the answers I was after," Luke said, starting to set the broken ancile on the bench beside him.

A strange, distant voice whispered words through the air beneath the hood. "Hold the weapon a while longer, for I am Rufus."

Luke stopped himself before dropping it to the bench. "You can speak?"

"Yes," Rufus, the shade, said. "I have traveled a long way to bring that to you, Luke Valor."

Luke lifted his eyebrows. The shade knew his name. Not a good sign. "Guess we'll start with how you know my name."

"There are a many great things I know about you. For I share fragmented thoughts with the one you call Aurelia, the one who cares deeply for you," Rufus said. "It took time for me to sort through our connection, but eventually it became clear to me, and I made my way to you."

This was the first time Luke had anyone talk about Aurelia, and this shade was somehow connected to her. "What have you done to her?" He stood up, lifting the ancile at him.

A harsh, distant laugh echoed from underneath the hood. "It isn't about what I have done but about what she has done." Rufus continued with anger in his voice, "That cursed woman destroyed my life's work and shattered my soul."

Luke remembered details about the mission that Aurelia had been sent on. "Are you saying that you are Evocator Rufus?" he asked.

"Yes, the one and the same." The shade bobbed up and down as if bowing.

Luke's mother was right. They needed to destroy this

cursed thing. If the Evocator, which Aurelia had gone to stop, was here now, it wasn't good.

"I think you've answered everything I needed to know." Luke picked up the cloth and began to wrap it around the broken ancile.

"Stop! You can still save her…" The shade shimmered in place as it screamed at him.

Luke had moved quicker when the shade screamed, but the last words caught his ear. He stopped himself from unwrapping it again and set it down on the bench.

"OK, you need to slow down," he told himself. His thoughts were racing. The shade had just said that he could still save her. What did he mean by that, and would he really be willing to sacrifice his part in protecting the realm by hearing out the one person who had tried to destroy the realm three years ago?

When Luke had investigated the disappearance of Lady Aurelia, the details arose on Evocator Rufus. He had woven evil works of darkness into the fabrics of the realm, not only with the Inmortuae but also with the Daemons.

Rufus made pacts with the Daemons allowing them into the realm, and with the help from the Forsvar, they had been able to thwart the Daemons, and that left only Evocator Rufus to deal with. Aurelia, along with a small legion, had gone after him.

Now Rufus was bound within the broken ancile he had given to Aurelia, and he possibly had the answer to what happened to her. There was a risk of him putting the realm in danger again, and whatever Aurelia had done would be lost.

But Luke couldn't let himself go with more unanswered questions. He tossed the cloth aside and gripped the broken ancile.

The shade appeared once more, and Luke looked straight at it. "First, I have some questions."

"I'll answer only that which is beneficial to me," Rufus spoke.

"Were you the one following me?"

"To an extent."

"What does that mean?"

"Beneficial only to myself. Please continue with your questions," Rufus said, leaving the first question unanswered.

"Are you bound to follow this broken ancile?" Luke asked.

"My soul was severed and bound to this cursed weapon you hold in your hand, though…" The voice dropped under the hood. "Do please continue."

Luke felt like Rufus was withholding information at the last moment, only mentioning small details that wouldn't be of any benefit.

He wanted to ask more questions, but one was the most important of all. "Can I still save Aurelia?"

The shade hovered for what seemed like hours to Luke, but the voice came again from the hood. "Yes."

"How?"

"Enough with your questions. Take me to Rubrum Castellum, and we'll continue once we've arrived."

Luke felt that it was a trick. "Why Rubrum Castellum? Why don't you tell me how to save her and we skip going to a place that fell into ruins?"

The air in the room chilled, and the shade appeared to grow in size. "Bound I may be to that cursed weapon, yet my powers reach well beyond such mortal understanding."

Luke could see his breath come out in smoky puffs in the suddenly chill room. He began to place the broken ancile down on the bench to avoid dealing any longer with the shade.

"I do not fear you, Luke, legionnaire of Arcem Regni. I have found others within Aurelia's fragmented thoughts that love and hold her dearly to their hearts. You were just the first of many attempts to manifest myself back in the flesh, and if you choose now to not save your precious lady of the realm, others may be so inclined to do so." The shade hovered, hissing through the freezing cold air. Then he whispered as he approached Luke. "Such as her sister, Beatrix."

Luke dropped the broken ancile from his hand at the last word, and the chill started to fade from the room.

He needed to destroy the ancile, right now, before anyone got hurt. Rufus was not to be messed with, and Aurelia had already saved the realm. But how could he remain faithful to his promises to protect the realm when he was offered the chance to bring Aurelia back?

The conflict between right and wrong lay before him. Aurelia had given her life in defense of the realm to stop a madman from unleashing havoc and destruction upon it. Was he willing to undo it all by listening to Rufus in order to save her?

Luke's thoughts fell on Beatrix. He wasn't going to let Rufus go after her. He decided to see what more Rufus had to say but stopped himself from picking up the broken ancile when the door opened across the room.

Marius and Beatrix entered, closing the door behind them.

Chapter 6: The Mission and Oaths

The three of them stared at each other, neither wanting to say the first word. Tension filled the room.

Marius and Beatrix both stared around the room. Beatrix rubbed the sides of her arms, feeling the chill.

"It's colder in here than usual," she said, finally breaking the ice.

Luke looked over at her. He did not want to give any details on what had happened to make the room so cold, so he tried to play it off. "I felt the cold air when he walked in."

Marius grinned. "Levelheaded even when you're under house arrest, stubborn to the end. Like father like son."

"Wouldn't want to let him down." Luke smiled back.

"Trying to live up to your father's name? Well you have a long way to go to accomplish that," Marius said. "Heh, I should try to be like good old Nero."

Luke's smile faded. Marius had grown up and fought beside his father in the previous war with the Daemons, working alongside the Forsvar. If Marius wasn't even close to being like his father, what chances did Luke have?

"At least you knew who he was," Luke said.

"That's your problem, feeling sorry for yourself when

everyone else is suffering around you. Nero didn't have a selfish bone in his body," Marius scolded.

"General Marius, if you'd please," Beatrix cut in. "We came here with a plan, and all you two can do is speak to one another that way. Let us continue with why we came."

Marius bowed his head, waving his hand toward Luke for agreement. Luke nodded, and Marius spoke. "Lady Ursus worries that if you do not attend the investigation, you won't let it go." Luke wanted to talk, but Marius raised his hand and continued. "She has decided to allow a small group of Ancilians, including Beatrix and I, to investigate your findings. After the incident, Lord Ursus's physician concluded that we have close to four weeks before his passing. That leaves us with very little time to finish the investigation and get you back and ready for the coronation."

Marius waved his hand at Beatrix and Luke. "That includes the two of you and a handful of Ancilian legions to protect the future lord and lady of the realm, which is rather insane. Still, Beatrix insisted on not leaving you alone, and without further argument, it was settled."

Beatrix and Luke smiled at each other. He did think that having her come with them would be rather dangerous, but the realm had been at peace for a while now.

"That is why I'm coming. It is my duty to protect the realm, and that means following you at the moment. Our duty shall be to protect Lady Scorpio before assisting you, if any danger comes our way." Marius smirked at Luke. "Though I may send a legionnaire or two to help you out if it comes to that."

Beatrix touched his arm, and Marius's smirk faded. "I jest, but you heard the lady of the realm. Any questions?"

It had happened so quickly. One moment Luke was under house arrest, and the next, they were preparing to go with him. He wanted to know why. "Why the change of heart?"

"As I said before, you won't ever get past the fact that someone missed something, and Lady Ursus needs you to focus on your duty to the realm, not on something in the past."

Luke wanted to protest against it being in the past. It was the first clue they had in a while, and she was alive; at least he knew she was because of the conversation with Rufus—which he wasn't going to bring up now. They were going to go to Rubrum Castellum, and he'd get more answers from Rufus there.

"Was it all about me leaving it in the past, or was there more to it?" Luke asked.

"Heh," Marius said, something he always did when

trying to bite his tongue. "It has been a long time since we've seen anything of Lady Aurelia's, and the queen was rather insistent that we check it out. Against my better wishes."

"Closure is what Marius means to say," Beatrix explained. "The realm needs closure on Lady Aurelia, and if this helps everyone find out a little more about what happened to her, then it is worth the trouble. There are strict terms that will allow us to continue, and you must agree to them before we proceed."

Luke knew those were coming. It was an agreement that would hold him to the highest degree if he were to stray from the mission. Not only would he be called a deserter, but he would also be held accountable for his actions.

"Would you like us to continue with the terms?" Beatrix asked, her face held firm in question. She knew him and didn't want him to agree to something if he would ignore them.

Luke stared back at her. It was the only way he would get his answers. "Yes, milady."

"Luke Valor, as an officer in the Ancilian legion, do you swear on your own honor that you will follow your commander? You will obey orders and without question. You will relinquish the protection of the realm and accept the power of your commander to put you to death without trial for disobedience or desertion. You will serve the realm faithfully, even at the cost of your life, and will respect the law with regards to your fellow Ancilians and legionaries. Do you swear?"

"I swear." Luke bowed. He had answered this when joining the ranks of the legion.

"Your commander will be Marius Wilhelm, general of the realm. Do you swear to follow your commander?" she continued.

"I swear." He saw the smug look on Marius's face, but he had already promised to follow him previously.

"Do you, Marius Wilhelm and Luke Valor, swear to follow my command as the future lady of the realm and your commanding officer on this mission?"

Marius was caught off guard slightly by her question. Luke smiled a bit. Then they both swore to follow her.

"Good. Now to the last term." Beatrix cleared her throat and then continued, "Do you swear to uphold your oaths, regardless of the outcome of this mission?"

Luke started to speak and then wondered which oaths she referred to but decided not to ask. "I swear."

Beatrix let out a sigh of relief. "That concludes the terms—rather simple but necessary in these circumstances. We set out first thing in the morning." She opened the door and left.

"Let this mission put the past to rest. The realm needs strong and honorable leaders." Marius paused, lowering his head. "I know what it does to a man when he never lets the past be."

Luke wanted to let go of the past and move on as well, but without knowing what happened to her, he wasn't going to be able to let it go. He desperately hoped they'd find her. "I hope that this is the last time we go searching for Lady Aurelia," he said, lifting the cloth and wrapping the broken ancile in in. No need to have the shade spook him in front of Marius.

"Agreed. Everyone needs closure on this," Marius said.

Luke gathered what he needed and started for the door, where Marius still stood at attention. He lifted his hand to stop Luke before letting him go.

"Do you know why she asked you about your oaths?" Marius asked, then continued. "She was worried that if you find Aurelia, it would mean the end of your courtship. I'll remember the oaths you swore on this day, and I'll hold you accountable for each and every one." He pressed against Luke and turned for the door.

Luke knew there was some reason she had asked him about his oaths, but he didn't know what it would mean for Beatrix and him if they found Aurelia. What would the future be like if they found Aurelia and brought her home? Could he be faithful to the oaths he had made to Beatrix?

Chapter 7: Departing Arcem Regni

Luke gathered his birrus and ancilia before he walked out into the dark-set sky. The rain had settled down, and the dark clouds still covered most of the light cast by the moon and stars. He paused before the statue of Aurelia and found himself gazing at the water surrounding her, gently rippling from the light drops hitting the surface.

He hoped that he wouldn't have to see a statue to remember who she was and that she would be coming home. With the cloth still tight in his grip, he could feel the sense that there was truth to Rufus's words. He could still save her, and the answers were at Rubrum Castellum.

Luke found his steps lighter than before as he passed the forge and made his way home for the night.

Slowly, he opened the door to his home and stared into the lightly lit kitchen. His mother was sitting up with her ancilia in her hands. Once she saw him, she dropped the ancilia and hit the covers. "We'll talk in the morning," she said, going to sleep for the night. He closed the door, knowing that any sound he made couldn't wake her from where she walked in her dreams.

Ever since he was a child, trying to find comfort from

his parents after he had a nightmare was impossible. Their bodies were there, and he could see them breathing, but trying to wake them never worked.

Questions like this were why he wanted his mother to tell him what had happened to his father. He knew his father hadn't always been a Forsvar like his mother, but she hadn't told him how it happened, and the details from Marius were limited.

Seeing his mother toss and turn reminded him of the horrors he had faced when seeing his father awaken with new scars upon his face or broken bones that needed to be set. His mother said it was the way of the Forsvar, and she would awaken in a panic, asking where he was or had been. She was determined to find him and bring him home.

It was all very confusing to him as a child and didn't make much sense even now.

Marius said Nero had charged head-on into the Daemon plane of existence and returned with Luke's mother and newly set spikes in his shoulder. Spikes that caused him to dream like the Forsvar.

What did the spikes do? Why did he have them? More unanswered questions. He knew that every Forsvar he had ever seen wore spikes similar to those his father and mother had on their shoulders. It had to do something with the spikes in their shoulders that had caused his father to fall apart, forcing him to be like the

Forsvar, stuck between the two realms.

That was what Luke wanted to know. What was it all about? The spikes, the walking in another realm.

Luke crossed over to the closet and opened it to see the armor once more. He reached over to the shoulders of the armor and felt the large holes dented inward. That was where the spikes were driven into his father, prompting his slow decline into madness and eventually his death. He wrapped his hands around the cloth carrying the broken ancile and tossed it into the closet. *Hopefully it's safe here*, he thought to himself.

He closed the wooden doors and walked to the main door, ensuring it was locked from within. He needed to protect his mother. Whenever they were in this state, they were vulnerable to the outside world. That is why she had sat up waiting for him to return before sleeping for the night.

Frustrated that he was spinning his thoughts back into the unanswered questions, he poured himself a glass of water from the pitcher.

He kicked off his boots, setting aside his birrus, armor, and ancilia before lying in his bed. He found the covers comforting as he pulled them over his chest and shoulders. The excitement of leaving tomorrow for Rubrum Castellum consumed his thoughts, and eventually, he found himself asleep.

Luke had been in a deep sleep when his mother shook him. "Wake up—we need to discuss what happened last night."

He was finally able to get himself out of bed and detail what happened in the lord and lady's house, his house arrest, and he trusted her to talk about Rufus's shade.

"You never should have touched that thing in the first place. Where did you put it? We need to destroy it before you leave." she said, shuffling through his things. "Where did you put it?"

"Mother, I put it with father's things in the closet," Luke said, moving out of the bed. "We can't destroy it until I figure out what happened at Rubrum Castellum."

"If that truly is Rufus's shade, then we got all we needed from him. You can find your own way about the ruins without him." She tossed open the closet and saw the cloth sitting at the bottom of the closet. She picked up the cloth and rushed it over to the door, then returned to the closet and started touching everything within.

"What are you doing?" Luke asked, seeing her look around as she touched each object in the closet.

"Making sure that cursed man didn't split his soul and curse your father's things," she said, moving her hand to another article in the closet, then stared around.

"He could do that?"

"That madman has done worse," she said, continuing her work, and then closed the closet's wooden doors.

"We can't destroy it. Rufus said I could still save her," Luke said, shifting his armor back into place and putting on his boots.

His mother turned and glared at him; her dark-brown eyes blazed with a kind of determination within that scared Luke. "Do you know what you are asking of your mother?"

He cleared his throat and continued to stare at the fiery determination within her eyes. "Trust."

The fire burned out, and she walked over to a chair and fell into it. "He used to say those exact words to me. Trust." She choked back the heartache.

Luke moved over to the table and sat beside his mother, reaching out, touching her shoulder, avoiding the spike. "Mother, it's the only way we're going to get the answers we need."

"At what cost?" she asked, touching his hand. "He'll want something in return, and what are you willing to sacrifice for her?"

Luke looked back at his mother and didn't have the words for what she asked. What was he willing to sacrifice for Aurelia? His own life, if needs be. Would it require him to lose others? What would it cost the realm? He thought of Beatrix and didn't have the words for his mother.

"I know what you're thinking, that he sacrificed everything for the realm and me. Don't lose your life the way he did." She had tears running down her face. "I know that I said you weren't ready, but maybe when you return we can revisit my past and I'll tell you what happened to your father. He would have wanted that, especially for his son."

Luke felt a bit of happiness flood his mind. A lot was happening, and he thought that it was about time to get the answers he'd been seeking for.

They sat there for a moment before Luke started to pack a few of his things for the road. "Are you going to be fine while I'm away?" Luke said, pushing things into a pack.

"I won't be here," his mother responded. "There are some things I need to take care of, and I can't do them here."

Luke stopped and looked at his mother. "Where are you going?"

"Can't tell you where I am going."

Luke rolled his eyes, another element of mystery in his life. He continued to pack his things. "I would ask why, but I fear I already know the answer to that question."

"Did Marius talk to you about the trouble with the Daemons?" Her voice was calm.

Luke remembered that Lady Ursus had told him to be filled in on the details from Marius, but he hadn't had the time. "Not yet. I was supposed to check in with Marius today about it."

"Make sure he gives you all the details, tell him that Cassia says he better." She stood up and walked to the chest beside her bed, lifting out her own pack. "Things are getting worse with the Daemons, and the likelihood of another invasion will be quickly upon us."

"I'll make sure he knows to fill me in on all the details," he replied.

She stopped and moved over to him and lifted his chin into her hands. "Promise me that no matter what he says, you'll push and push. He'll only tell you what he feels you need to know, and there is always more, always."

"I got it." Luke shook his face out of his mother's grasp and went to the kitchen to put food in his pack.

"Are you going to take your father's armor on this mission?" she asked across the room, and it caught Luke off guard as it always did.

He wasn't ready to put that armor on or use his

ancilia. It wasn't the right time for him, but it never stopped his mother from asking.

"I'm not ready," he replied, like he always did.

She sighed, but this time didn't let it go. "There are things I'll keep from you until you are ready." Luke looked at her, and she nodded his way. "Mothers always have a way to keep their children on their toes."

Luke let out a sad laugh and knew his mother was right.

They finished packing their things and headed for the door. "I'll have the apprentices at the forge look over our home while we are away, but with it being close to the castle. I doubt anyone will try anything," his mother said as they glanced back at the belongings in their home.

Luke looked back and felt that it might be a long time before he was safe within these walls.

They turned and closed the door behind them, each leaving on a journey of their own making.

Chapter 8: Journey to the Ruins

The legion set out upon the roads leading out of the great city of Arcem Regni. The rain had made the roads muddy, and it slowed their march, but without a cloud in sight, the sun started to dry all the water from the heavy rainfall.

Beatrix led at the front alongside Marius while Luke rode behind with his legionaries. Each had been assigned ten soldiers spread out in five rows of two. The columns behind Beatrix and Marius were twenty soldiers spread out in two columns of five rows of two. The last column followed behind Luke, and five scouts would report activity back to the legion outside of the marching legion.

Thirty-five Ancilian soldiers had been assigned to this mission, and they made their march southeast toward the ruins of Rubrum Castellum.

There was plenty of time to think during the march, and Luke spent his time trying to piece things together.

Three years ago, Lady Aurelia had made her last mission out to Rubrum Castellum to stop Evocator Rufus. Reports came in that an Evocator was using magic, opening ways into the realm for the Daemons to enter.

Evocators were known for their magic with the

Inmortuae, the undead. They could conjure the spirits of the dead or animate the dead into creatures of dark and ill intent. The Inmortuae were irritating to the Ancilians, but their numbers were never enough to cause a war. Legions would be dispatched to quell an uprising or reported Evocator, and most Evocators had learned to use their magic for purposes of revealing a loved one or trying to influence the course of events.

However, when the reports and numbers of the Daemon rose exponentially, which were traced back to Evocator Rufus, it was unknown how he had opened a way for the Daemons. Still, with the help of the Forsvar, the Ancilians, along with Aurelia's last mission, had put an end to the conflict.

When Luke had gone out to find Aurelia after the siege upon the walls had ended, all they found was the city of Rubrum Castellum in ruins. A city built during the war with the Daemons overlooked the valley below. That war ended seventeen years ago. Luke had been five at the time.

It was now in ruins; stones were scattered around the encampment, and the city had disappeared entirely. They had found legion equipment and piles of bones but none of the missing legionaries or Aurelia.

Determined to find her, he had scouted the place for days, hoping that something would turn up. He dug through the dirt around the area, finding nothing useful. Eventually, they left the site, and now with newfound information, they returned once again.

Luke didn't expect to find anything that they hadn't seen before, but with the help of Rufus's shade, he felt hopeful they would find something new.

Continuing to put the pieces together after her mission, they spent the next three years scouring the realm for her. They went place after place but found no news about her disappearance. Once in the Port of Cymatilis, they heard rumors of an Ancilian soldier arriving at the port after the quakes had occurred. Searching the port, they had found only Ancilian equipment belonging to one of their previous officers, Felix Rius. Continuing their search never bore fruit.

The clues or rumors of sightings throughout the realm became a hindrance to their investigation, and slowly they stopped believing them.

Luke had tried his best to help his mother produce more ancilia at the forge when he was home, but whenever he got the chance to go out to find Aurelia, he went.

Everyone had been supportive and acknowledged his determination to find Aurelia. They all wanted to bring her home. A day had turned into a week, weeks into a month, and months into a year. Slowly they grew weary and undetermined to take up the search.

Luke was persistent, and one by one, everyone had given up. Lord and Lady Ursus knew that their daughter wouldn't want them to let the realm fall apart without her. Aurelia had given everything she had to the realm. The realm came first in everything she did, and with that, her parents pushed to rebuild the realm to what it was before the Daemon invasions.

They built the statue of their daughter and called her the hero of the realm, breathing new hope and life into the city as they tried to stop the mourning and bring light into the dark place it had been for the last three years.

Feeling alone in his determination to find Aurelia had been the fire Luke needed to go on, and he woke up hoping to find that new piece that would bring her home. Three years later, and he had finally found it.

It was easier to confide in Beatrix than anyone else about Aurelia because of their childhood. Beatrix had been adopted into the Ursus family during the Daemon wars after her family was killed during the invasions. The legionaries had brought home refugees from the burnt-down cities around the realm. Beatrix was among them.

The Ursus family was focused intently on protecting the realm, with Nero and Marius leading the effort, and had decided their daughter Aurelia needed family companionship during these challenging times. With that thought, they had welcomed Beatrix into their family.

When Luke had been left behind, the Ursus family had allowed him to stay within the main keep walls while his father and mother went out to war. He had become close friends with Aurelia and Beatrix during that time, and they grew up together.

Though they thought of Luke as their brother, Aurelia had started to have feelings for the young Valor and would find a way to show her emotions toward him during their training.

The three of them had remained close throughout the wars and their young adult lives. Luke had left on assignment with the legion to learn his duties to the realm in his youth, with very little time left to spend with Aurelia.

Beatrix had joined the legions with him, where they had learned to sign. The signing was one of the ways the Forsvar spoke with the Ancilians and among each other. Nero and Marius had led that charge when they joined up with the Forsvar during the war.

Though he had spent most of the time with Beatrix in the Legions, he would often think of Aurelia and wonder what she was up to back at Arcem Regni.

In the weeks leading up to the last invasion on Arcem Regni, Aurelia had made it known that she had picked Luke to join her in succession to become lady and lord of the realm. She expressed her opinions openly, stating that he was the son of the great hero Nero Valor and had led an exemplary tenure in the legion.

Luke spent most of his time courting Aurelia before the last invasion upon the city until she was called out on her mission.

His questions about why she had picked Felix to accompany her over him went unanswered. The Ursuses stated that it was her decision as the commander on the mission, and that was that.

Devastated, he pushed himself harder than he ever had before, and his dedication to the realm started to lack, which was why Marius had been so disappointed in him recently. Through it all, he found himself more and more in the presence of Lady Beatrix at home. She would just sit and listen to him. At the end of these last three years, she had started to show feelings for him. At first, he thought she was simply feeling pity for him, feeling the loss of her sister, but eventually, they talked about it.

Then when Lord Ursus's health started fading, it was decided that a new lord and lady were needed to lead the realm together. Beatrix became that successor, and Luke was dragged into it with her.

Once again, the details of Luke's heritage and past

deeds made him worthy of joining Lady Beatrix in leading the realm with the assistance of Lady Ursus.

The courtship of Luke and Beatrix had just begun, one they had both agreed they should take slow but was now being rushed.

They were told to show commitment to each other whenever they could in front of the Ancilians, even if it was hard. Lady Ursus was very opinionated on how she wanted things done. Being the friends they were, Luke and Beatrix had first started to make jokes about it, but Lady Ursus quickly stopped that nonsense.

The day had set further into the afternoon as they continued their journey along the roadway, and Luke found himself eager to speak with Beatrix after concluding his thoughts.

Luke told the soldier at the front of the column that he was heading to speak with Lady Scorpio, and he was in charge until he returned. He then kicked his horse, urging it forward.

"Have a moment to talk?" Luke asked as he arrived in step with Beatrix.

Beatrix turned toward him and smiled. "Yes." She motioned for Marius to take charge of the two columns as she moved her horse outside the columns beside Luke and his horse.

Beatrix spoke when they were sure that they could

talk privately with all the horses and Legions in lockstep. "What took you so long? There is only so much I can talk to Marius about, and I swear he enjoys just mumbling to himself. I was losing my mind. Anyway, how are you?"

"Sorry about that. I fell right into Legion modus, walking aimlessly with only my thoughts. There is quite a bit to think about these days," he replied. "Other than having no answers to my questions, I'm doing OK."

"Always good having a chance to clear your head. I've been thinking about my discussion with my mother." Beatrix looked to the sides to make sure no one could hear her. "She was telling me that there had to be an insider who had slowly infected my father. Can you believe it? Someone close has been doing this to him. Makes me sick just thinking about it."

Luke watched as Beatrix shook her head in disgust, his own thoughts trying to put the pieces together. "There are only a handful of people who have been close to Lord Ursus over the years; they have to be able to narrow it down."

"Yes, but she has only brought in Marius, me, and now you. She isn't willing to share it beyond that in hopes they can find the individual before they try something else," Beatrix replied. She raised her eyebrows at Luke. "That was why Marius was very bitter toward you last night, with everything going on. This was just another thing to take away from what the realm really needed."

Luke lowered his head for a moment and understood Marius's attitude toward him last night. Still, he felt like no one cared about finding Aurelia, and he had to try whenever he could. "Didn't mean for it to happen the way it did, but when I found…"

"Her missing blade, you felt that we needed to investigate," Beatrix cut him off. "Marius filled me in on the details of why we're on this mission in the first place, and I need to be honest with you, Luke. It wasn't exactly what I had in mind when I told you I didn't want to be confined to those walls any longer."

"You did tell me that I should have taken you on my last mission." Luke smiled.

"Technically yes, but I honestly was trying to hint that what I really needed was to get out."

"And here we are." He waved his arms to the open space around them.

"I think I'd rather listen to Marius grumbling than your nonsense right now." Beatrix started to move her horse toward the legions and then stopped. "Never mind. I don't think I can take much more of it. Guess I'm stuck with you, literally."

They laughed together, which felt good for Luke

since the past day had given him too many other things to think about. It felt good to get out and just talk.

"The legions were tough, and there were times when I thought I wasn't going to make it home," Luke said. "Now, thinking about the responsibility of the realm being held over my head, I'd rather be fighting for my life."

"Oh, you don't know the half of it," Beatrix said. "If I find myself in one more of those dresses, I am going to lose it. Give me my ancilia and armor, and I feel like I belong. Back there playing lady of the realm, I can't be myself."

"Can't someone else be interim lord and lady for a while?" Luke joked.

"That is the kind of nonsense my mother is sick of," Beatrix stated firmly with tight lips, which she then relaxed into a smile. "Without Aurelia, they are stuck with me, and I thought, well, misery likes company, so why not bring you along?"

Luke shook his head. "You're funny."

"I know." She smiled back at him.

The legions slowed their march, and they saw Marius raising his hand for them to stop. One of the scouts was heading quickly in their direction, dust kicking up off the roadway as he made his approach.

"Report, soldier," Marius asked as the scout

approached.

"A group of Forsvar have requested to speak with you, General," the soldier responded.

"Allies?" Marius asked.

"I was told to give you this." The soldier held out a piece of parchment, and Marius grabbed it.

Beatrix and Luke had made their way back into the circle with Marius. Beatrix requested to see the parchment. Marius handed it to her, saying, "Won't mean much to your eyes."

She read the parchment and looked back at him. "What does this symbol mean?"

Beatrix held it out for Luke to see.

It was symbol Luke had only seen on his father's armor. A rising phoenix from the ashes, though this one had spikes drawn into the shoulders of the phoenix, along with a few markings that meant nothing to him.

"The symbols mean something to me," Marius said.

"Keeping secrets, general?" Beatrix piped up.

Marius reached for the parchment. "It means they're our allies. I'll speak with them and report back, commander."

"See what they want," Beatrix said.

Marius nodded his head and went out with the soldier to meet the Forsvar.

Beatrix looked at them go and then turned to Luke.

"Was going to suggest joining him, but I felt like he wanted to go alone."

"What makes you say that?" Luke asked.

"He resents that I am in command of this outfit, and he only offered himself to go out to speak with them."

Luke reflected on Marius's tone and words and could see how she had come to that conclusion. The symbol was where his thoughts had been, the same as one on his father's armor but slightly different.

Marius had mentioned the word *allies* since not all of the Forsvar were working with the Ancilians. There were Forsvar hostile to the Ancilians and those working with the Daemons.

Beatrix commanded the legions to continue their march toward Rubrum Castellum, knowing that Marius would eventually catch up. "No need to wait needlessly," she told Luke as they continued on.

"Why would the Forsvar be this far out into the open? Most of them don't come out this far into the realm," Luke wondered aloud to Beatrix as they marched on.

"Not sure. Let's see what Marius reports back."

Luke made his way back to his column to get a status report while waiting for Marius to return. Then he placed the front soldier back in charge and headed to the front as he saw Marius returning.

"They are meeting up with a few of the Forsvar from the city," Marius said.

Luke instantly wondered about his mother. "Was my mother with them?"

"No, but she was one of the ones they were waiting for," he replied. "They also report some abnormal activity out on the roads and that we should be careful."

Beatrix thanked Marius for the report, and they returned to their formation and continued the march.

Luke told Beatrix he'd be back to keep her company later and moved his way back to his column. He thought more about the symbol of the phoenix rising from the ashes; it symbolized a new beginning, but it wasn't worn by the other Ancilians. He did see it on that parchment Marius had received, and his mother was going out to meet the Forsvar.

Piece by piece, he'd find a way to see how it all fit together.

Chapter 9: Questions at Camp

Dusk set in as the sun dipped beyond the western mountains. In the distance to the east, they could see the mountains that circled about, creating Vallis Ossa, the valley of bones. Once a valley of beauty, now a wasteland scattered with bones of fallen Ancilians, Forsvar, and Daemons during the wars from Nero and Marius's time.

The ruins of Rubrum Castellum stood upon the mountains overlooking the valley. Their destination was far but visible in the distance.

Each column from the legion unpacked their assigned mule, unfolding the leather roof and setting the tent poles, pegs, and ropes into place. The tents were set up close together and could hold each column of soldiers. Their extra weapons had been placed behind the tents, and the officers drew smaller tents for their quarters.

They wouldn't be staying here longer than the night and decided they could hold their conversations around the fire without the need to set up the officer's quarters, where they could stand and discuss mission details from within the tent.

The officers' tents had enough room to slide under, which provided protection from the outside elements but not much space to do anything else but sleep.

With the soldiers' tents set on the west side of camp, fires scattered in the center, and the officers' tents on the east side, they settled in for the night.

The soldiers unwound from the long journey, telling stories and warming some of the extra food the mules had carried with them.

Luke found Beatrix outside her tent, away from the soldiers, sitting against her pack. "Finding a quiet place away from all the noise?" he asked, settling on the ground beside her.

"Not quiet enough." Beatrix stared at the soldiers enjoying their night with loud voices and laughter. They weren't that far from the others.

"At least it's away from most of the commotion." Luke could see she was deep in thought. "What's on your mind?"

Her finger dragged in the dirt, creating circles and random symbols. "Don't want you worrying about it."

Luke knew Beatrix enough that if he pushed, she'd tell him. She had always been up-front with him, but it was clear that she wanted to let her thoughts gather before she spoke. So he let it go. "Tell me when you're ready," he assured.

"Thanks," she said, dusting herself off. "It's been a long day, and I'm going to turn in for the night. We'll be there a little after noon if we set out early enough."

Luke gazed up toward the Heavens. "I definitely need to get some sleep, but after all that rain we just had, it's nice to be able to look up at the night sky. The weather is almost perfect for camping underneath the stars, just not quite there yet."

She looked up toward the heavens with him. "It is a nice night, and I'd love to sit out here with you." She paused. "I've been trying to process the last day and a half, and it would be good to give my mind a break."

"Get some rest. I need to speak with Marius anyway," Luke said, standing up. "Is there anything I can do for you?"

"Not tonight. Good night," she said, moving into her tent, which was located in the center of the three officers' tents.

"Good night, Beatrix," he called after her and then went off to find Marius.

Luke found him talking to a handful of the soldiers around the fire and requested that they speak away from the others. After a moment, Marius excused himself, and they made their way to the south-side camp beside Marius's tent.

"Got something to say?" Marius asked when they were a reasonable distance away.

Luke wondered why Marius spoke to him that way

but let it go. "I wanted to ask you a few questions, starting with filling me in on the rumors of another Daemon invasion."

"Heh," Marius said. "The Forsvar have been sending us comprehensive reports on the activity within the Daemon realm. It reminded some of us old-timers that another invasion could be near at hand—though we don't have any way of knowing when it could begin, or where."

Lady Ursus hadn't given Luke any information about it. "Lady Ursus, said I should discuss this with you."

"Heh," Marius said again and then paused. "Preparations are already underway back at home. Officers were given their orders, and since this mission isn't over, there isn't much to discuss on the Daemon invasions."

"From your meeting with the Forsvar yesterday, there has been abnormal activity with the Daemons, and we should be prepared, if necessary, out on the road." Luke knew that there was more to discuss on the matter.

Marius waved his hand toward the soldiers in the encampment. "That is what this is all for. They are here to protect Lady Beatrix and for that matter, you. They aren't here on a routine training exercise; they came in case something goes bump in the night."

Luke could feel the tension rising between them, but

he wanted to know more about the Forsvar and why his mother had gone out with them. "Marius, I am just trying to understand the situation with the Forsvar better."

"Allegiances," Marius said. "Let me ask you a few questions before I elaborate on it for you. First, where does the alliance with the Forsvar stand with the Ancilians?"

Luke knew. He and Beatrix had been going over the realm's status over the past while as they prepared to become lord and lady of the realm. "Not holding as well as it should."

"Do you know why?"

"Over the last couple of years, more of our allies within the Forsvar have gone missing or silent."

"Exactly. Now why aren't we able to recruit more of the Forsvar to our cause?" Marius asked.

"We need our Forsvar allies to recruit their own to our cause," Luke said. He saw Marius waving his hand, urging him to continue. "And it isn't going well."

"Heh," Marius said and then paused in thought. "What do you know on what it takes to recruit the Forsvar to our cause?"

Luke didn't know much about what it took to recruit them or even find them. "Nothing, general."

Marius waited for another moment before saying,

"Heh, your mother hasn't told you anything."

Hearing about his mother reminded Luke he wanted Marius to fill him in on all the details of the invasion. "She said you'd fill me in on the details."

Marius furrowed his brow. "What details?"

Luke hoped he could get more than what his mother had told him to ask. "She said you had more information."

"I've been around a long time and could answer most of your questions. However, crossing Cassia isn't on my bucket list. Now, what did she want me to tell you?" Marius knew when to cross a line and when not to.

Luke wasn't going to get many answers this way. "The invasion."

"It's like I said: the invasion is being prepared back at the city—"

"She said to push until you gave me the details," Luke interrupted.

"Heh, good old Cassia." Marius thought for a moment before continuing. "I have other business to attend to this evening, but we can pick this up in the morning."

Luke knew it was over. "Until tomorrow. Good night, general."

Marius nodded his head, and they exchanged their

salutes.

Luke made his way to the tent to get ready for bed. He placed the cursed blade at the corner of the tent near his feet and settled. He couldn't stop thinking about what Marius had meant by other business, so he decided to see what Marius was up to.

The night had wound down, and most of the soldiers had made their way to their tents. A few stragglers sat around the fire, with a few already asleep. Others were on night watch.

Luke waited in his tent, watching Marius sitting contently outside his tent. He started to nod off a few times but caught himself. The next time he opened his eyes, he found Marius gone.

He lifted the flap of the tent, trying to find him. Then he went to the other side of the tent, lifting the flap to catch a glimpse of Marius standing outside the camp, waving his hands in the air.

There was a woman with him. Luke could see their hands moving back and forth, signing. He couldn't catch their words at this distance, but he could tell they knew each other.

Marius embraced the woman in a hug and gave her a kiss. Then he led her back to the camp. Luke could see the spikes set within the woman's shoulders. Her hair was tied back in a ponytail, with armor made of black linked chain mail and a long black cloak draped behind her. The night soldiers either ignored or hadn't seen her as she slipped into Marius's tent while Marius casually lay out under the starlight sky.

Luke had a hard time staying up any later. When he heard Marius's snores, he finally closed his own eyes. It wouldn't be long before they were under attack.

Chapter 10: The Inmortuae

Marius's voice called for battle, which sent shouts reverberating throughout the camp. Legionaries awoke to the attack upon their camp. Luke heard the shouting and started moving his way out of the tent, dragging his ancilia with him. The sun rose in the east and cast its rays upon the grounds surrounding the encampment.

It was being swarmed by the Inmortuae—undead creatures. The legionaries were engaged in combat, pushing to hold their ground around the camp. Only a handful of them were dressed in armor, while others wore the worn-out tunics they had slept in.

Two soldiers failed to move into formation and were being cut down by the crude weapons wielded by the Inmortuae. The legionaries pushed to surround their comrades, hoping to save their lives.

Skeletons carried crude spears, shivs made of bones, and their eyes glowed with blue fire. With a quick glance around the camp, Luke could see skeletons wearing discarded armor, others with their skin peeling off their bodies, wearing only cloth. The number of skeletons moving in on the camp was daunting to see. In the distance, he could see a hooded figure, with bones layered across his body and a lesser Daemon's skull upon his shoulder and a spike protruding out from the top of the skull. An Evocator. The Evocator sat upon a skeletal horse away from combat. A golem stood beside the Evocator and moved slowly toward the northern side of camp.

Luke gripped the handles of the ancilia, the shields covering his hands and wrists, and set out toward the nearest legionaries, with those from his column holding the northside.

A skeleton carrying shivs of bone saw Luke approaching and moved quickly toward him. Luke lifted his left arm, the shielded front facing the skeleton, leaving his stomach exposed and his right hand ready to strike.

He knew slashing the skeleton might be enough to break its bones, but he had other plans.

The shivs shot forward toward his stomach. He brought his left arm down, arced outward, and brought his right fist right through the skeleton's face. Without stopping his momentum, he shattered through the bones and continued past.

Another turned on his right, bringing his crude blade down toward his face. His right hand carried the forward momentum to his right, knocking the weapon aside, allowing his left arm to uppercut with his ancile to smash through the skeleton, crushing it to a pile of bones.

The legions brought their formation to a circle to protect one another from allowing their backs to be exposed. A few of the soldiers had discarded their second ancile in favor of a shield for protection. Luke knew that Marius's hard training had helped make the legionaries what they were today.

They had started to push their advance against the skeleton raid, shattering the bones and advancing step by step.

Luke slid in with his column and found a place between two shields. Whenever they saw an opening, the shields moved ever so slightly aside, allowing Luke to slide his weapon through to strike at the skeletons.

The golem slowly continued his approach as they downed the skeletons around them. It was covered with flesh and bones. The flesh pulled the bones around to form a body, sharp bones stuck out forming spikes, and where a face should be stood a cracked skull with blue orbs in the sockets. It stood at the height of a soldier sitting upon a large horse.

Soldiers were being jabbed at with bones through the onslaught. As one skeleton fell, another took its place, trying to find a way to break through the formation. With ten soldiers originally in his column, they were down to six, including Luke, holding the wall. It was enough to quell the assault.

"Pull back, and protect the wounded while we help

the others," Luke shouted above the din as the skeletons from the northside of the camp started to fall in numbers.

He turned to see Marius on the south side and his column holding out against the Inmortuae. He had done much better against them. He had all ten soldiers still standing.

Beatrix held her ground with her column beside Marius's, and they continued to hold the line.

"Marius, we're going to have a problem in a minute," Luke yelled to Marius, pointing at the golem about to enter the camp.

Marius grunted something, and his column surged forward, smashing the last of the skeletons, allowing them to turn and help Beatrix while he told three soldiers to head Luke's way.

"Break the line and set up in horned formation. Prepare to bring it down," Luke called out to the soldiers as they rushed to his column.

The soldiers began breaking into groups of three. The formation was set up for a soldier to be centered between two other soldiers with a shield. The other two soldiers extended their ancile out, making each group look like a bull.

Luke helped move the wounded farther into camp. Seizing the opportunity, the golem smashed his fist into the first group of legionaries. Two stood tightly behind the first, holding the shield as its fist hit the shield.

The soldier's arm would have broken under pressure, but in horned formation, the other two soldiers' weight and arms pressed against the shield, and it only pushed the group back a step.

The other groups pushed in, slashing their weapons against the flesh of the golem, sending bits and pieces flying to the ground. The rampage of the golem continued as it sent its fist flying toward the groups, but each time the soldiers held their ground. Just then, Luke caught a glimpse of a skeleton rising from his tent, holding a tightly wrapped cloth, and began sprinting toward the Evocator.

Luke was on the other side of the legionaries fighting the golem and would have to rush through to get to the skeleton in time; he had to stop himself from charging headlong to his death.

"Marius!" he yelled. "The Evocator—he's got Aurelia's ancile!"

Marius turned toward the rider, saw the skeleton running, and shrugged his shoulders at Luke, turning back to the fight in front of him.

Luke was frustrated and annoyed that he hadn't told Marius anything about the cursed weapon in the first place. That's why Marius had acted the way he did.

Luke sprinted around his column of legionaries, heading for his horse to catch the Evocator when one of the groups staggered backward to the ground. He turned; he couldn't leave his column now.

Ancilia in hand, he turned toward the golem and rushed toward it, connecting with the golem's wrist before it hit a soldier on the ground.

He felt his blades dig into the flesh of the golem's wrist and slam against the bone. He yelled, pushing harder through, bringing his blades upward to use the entire length of the blade, pressing against the weight of the golem.

This gave the soldiers enough time to pick themselves off the ground and move in against the golem's rage. Luke felt the pressure building and fell to his knees. His arms were giving out, and he knew the golem's fist would slam down at any moment.

Soldiers moved in beside Luke and lifted their own blades against the golem's flesh, distributing the weight off of Luke. The other two groups continued to take the brunt of the other fist and sliced their way into the golem's defenses. The golem lifted his wrist off the blades and sent it slamming down toward them.

Luke and the soldiers moved, avoiding the slam, and got back into formation. Luke glanced to the side and saw the Evocator heading southeast.

Marius and Beatrix had formed groups of three to push toward the golem and protect against its rampage. Its hands and feet connected against the shields, causing the legionaries to fall backward. They continued their assault against its flesh and worked their way down until the golem fell to the ground, no longer held together by its flesh.

Luke wanted to rush after the Evocator and get back the cursed blade, but he hadn't been expecting this. They had been ambushed, and who knew how many of their soldiers were going to make it?

They checked and attended to their wounded, finding that two soldiers in Luke's column had fallen in the battle with the Inmortuae.

They had been part of Luke's legionaries, and he prepared them for their eternal rest. His muscles were still shaking from holding the golem's wrist above his head, and he hadn't lost any soldiers in a long time. It pressed against his nerves, and he found himself suppressing his anger as he tossed the last of the dirt upon his fallen comrades.

They buried their soldiers in shallow graves and planned to retrieve their bodies on their way back home. For now, they would find rest until a proper burial could be given.

Beatrix knelt beside him. "There wasn't anything you could have done to save them. Your column's tent was closest to the conflict."

Luke looked up at her. "There had to be something I could have done."

Marius stepped up behind them, saluting the fallen soldiers. "Don't take the honor of the fallen; they gave their lives to the realm."

Luke stood up, turning to face Marius. "All I am saying is that I should have prepared for something like this to happen, but I didn't."

"Heh. None of us were prepared for what happened. What would you have done differently?" Marius asked.

Luke knew that he had been distracted the last day or so, concerned with finding Aurelia and the answers to his questions, and had stayed up later than he should have. If only he had gotten the needed rest, he wouldn't have been late to his column. "I had become too relaxed and thought it would be like the previous missions. I hadn't expected this."

"Heh." Marius left it at that.

Beatrix put her hand on his shoulder. "The realm isn't going to have the same peace anymore. There are things happening that are bigger than you and me. Whatever Aurelia did three years ago allowed the realm to have peace for a short time, but that's ending, and we need to be prepared for what's ahead."

"Don't beat yourself up. We all took a moment to

breathe after what Aurelia did. Lady Beatrix is right; we can't keep living the way we did," Marius said as he reached out and touched Luke's shoulder. "Strength and honor."

"Strength and honor," Luke replied. He felt better knowing he hadn't been the only one, but it continued to eat away at him.

Marius turned and left to break down the camp and put the packs on the mules.

"You going to be OK?" Beatrix asked, seeing Luke staring off into the distance.

"Yeah, might take some time. It's been a long time since we had a fight like that," Luke said, looking into her gentle blue eyes.

"We have a handful of hours before we reach Rubrum Castellum. Don't make me listen to Marius's grumbling for too long, and we can talk. How does that sound?"

"Sounds good to me."

Luke watched Beatrix head back toward the camp and help the soldiers finish up their duties. He had questions for Marius about who the woman was last night, but he'd wait. Right now, his eyes stared off into the distance where the Evocator had gone. They would be headed in the same direction, and Luke hoped he would get the chance to avenge his fallen comrades and get Aurelia's ancile back.

Chapter 11: Rubrum Castellum Ruinas

Marius instructed one of the scouts to return to Arcem Regni and request thirty more soldiers to be sent to Rubrum Castellum with detailed information on their fallen comrades. He requested that additional soldiers come and bring the fallen home.

Once they had broken down camp, they headed southeast toward Rubrum Castellum, leaving the battle behind them, unsure of what they were heading into.

Beatrix and Marius led their column forward, while Luke followed with the eight remaining soldiers in his column. The realm was warming up considerably, with the sun blaring in the sky and their late departure.

Once they had been on the road for a bit, with Rubrum Castellum close in sight, Luke dismissed himself and rode up beside Marius. "Have a moment?"

Marius glanced over to Beatrix, who waved him off and moved toward the center of both columns.

They rode off to the side and continued their march beside the columns. "I want to ask you about last night. After our discussion, I saw you with—"

Marius cut him off. "Let's move further out." After they moved farther away from the columns, he told Luke to continue.

"I saw you signing with a Forsvar woman last night,"

Luke told him point-blank.

"Heh, should have remembered that you're Nero's son, and nothing gets past you," Marius said.

"Who was she, and what did she want?" Luke asked.

"She needed a place to rest, and I offered her my protection for the night." Marius glared at him. "The same way you protect your own mother."

Luke told him about seeing him hug and kiss the woman, and Marius said nothing for a bit. It was a rather long and awkward pause.

"What do you know about the courtship between your mother and father?" Marius finally asked.

"I know the story about him charging in to save her." He tried to remember any other details he had learned along the way, but nothing stuck. "Not much else beyond him saving her."

"They knew each other way before that moment, and Cassia would hunt me down if I said anymore." Marius hesitated. "But as this relates to my situation, I am deeply in love with one of the Forsvar, like your father was. My situation is very different than Nero's, and last night was the first I had seen her in a long time. But even that brief moment gave me peace knowing she's alive."

Luke hadn't known that his mother and father were in love before he had saved her. It made sense why

Marius didn't have a wife back at home. He was in love with someone far from home.

"That's why I told you not to beat yourself up for earlier; we were all a bit distracted," Marius said. "One of these days, I'll have the courage to do what Nero did, but today isn't that day." He cleared his throat. "Anything else?"

"Yes, about Aurelia's blade—"

Marius interrupted him. "Don't worry about that thing. We don't need it to continue our investigation. That's why I shrugged it off. If some Evocator wants it, let him have it."

"The blade, it's…"

"You need to spend some time with Beatrix instead of this grumpy old man. Don't worry about the blade, we're already on the mission. It did its job," Marius said, riding back toward his column. He sent Beatrix out to meet Luke.

Luke had wanted to blurt out to Marius that it contained a piece of Rufus's soul, but he had been so quick to cut him off.

"How did your conversation go with Marius?" she asked, riding beside him. "The look on your face says it didn't go so well."

Luke shook his head and sat upright. "Was thinking about what he said to me."

"Which was?"

Luke tried to never have secrets between them, and the only one was the cursed blade that was now in the hands of the Evocator. He told her about the night prior and the woman Marius had met with. He went into detail about what he knew about his mother and father but found out there was more to be discovered.

"Marius is in love with a Forsvar woman?" Beatrix said out loud, and Luke had to shush her. "It makes so much sense now. All these years of him without a wife and focusing solely on the legionaries' training…"

"I know."

"Why doesn't she live with him? Your mother moved into the city and ran the forge with your father, so why doesn't she do the same?"

"He didn't say," Luke replied. He had wondered the same thing, but Marius hadn't said anything about it.

"Maybe I can get him to divulge those secrets to me when I am officially lady of the realm." She laughed. "Can you imagine the look on his face?"

"He'd blame me for telling you." Luke laughed with her.

"Question the lady and lord of the realm? I don't think he'd do that," she said sarcastically.

That's when the ground shook momentarily. They looked at each other and took off to the front of the columns with Marius.

Clouds began forming over Rubrum Castellum. They swirled about, blue streaks filling the clouds before slowly descending toward the ruins.

"Whatever that is, it's trouble. We need to get there now and stop it," Marius said. He ordered the soldiers to move at a faster pace.

The ground shook again, and Luke went to his column, ordering them to press forward behind the others. The clouds continued their descent, and the quakes became more frequent.

They arrived on the outskirts of Rubrum Castellum, the clouds roaring above their heads. They could see the ruins were now being filled with a structure from underground. The building rose slightly above the earth with each quake, sending dust and rocks scattering.

The Evocator who had attacked them that morning stood in the ruins. One hand was held against his side while the other conducted the magic. Blue fire danced in his hand, and out to the sides of him, three large hounds pushed through the dirt, their claws digging their way out.

Glowing red eyes, a fiery red mouth, canine teeth, and fangs extended over the lips. Their faces were bone, with wavy blue ethereal strands flying behind their heads. Each vertebra along the back extended out beyond the flesh, and mangled black fur was stretched beyond, exposing the fire beneath.

They stood above the waist of the Evocator, who had his back still turned.

On the outskirts of the ruins, the Inmortuae began to form. The skeletons cracked their bones into place with glowing blue eyes, and the Inmortuae moved toward them.

"Commander, may I?" Marius requested charge of the battle from Beatrix. She nodded, and he continued. "Daemon hounds." He lowered himself from his horse. "Form up and prepare to hold the line. If one of these things gets past you, don't try fighting it alone. Its speed and strength will rip your throat in moments."

The columns started to form up with their officers and prepared for battle. "Luke, your column is to stop the Evocator's incantation; if he is allowed to finish, who knows what will happen?" Marius said, "We'll press forward against the hounds and Inmortuae."

Luke turned toward his column, waving them to the north, away from the other two columns. "We're going in with horn formation. Always face the hound and take it down."

"There are only eight of us, sir," one of the soldiers

said.

"I know. I'm going as one of the horns." Luke slid one of his ancilia back into its sheath and lifted his right blade as they broke into formation. He stepped in line behind the soldier with the shield and took the right side.

"When the other columns move, we go in with them."

The Inmortuae and hounds waited. The hounds paced back and forth, glowing red eyes watching the advance of the Ancilians.

The ground began to shake, and the hounds leaped off the ground. Their speed was incredible. Within seconds, two had covered the distance, slammed against Beatrix's formation, and broken through the shield wall, sending soldiers flying to the side.

One hound directed its attention toward Luke's column and tried to come in on the side of one of the horned groups.

The group moved together as one, and the hound slammed, leaving claw marks down the face of the shield, and bounded back before the soldier's blades found their mark.

It eyed the soldiers and howled. Skeletons turned and moved toward the howling, and as the hound backed away, they moved past to engage the soldiers.

"We're moving to the front," Luke said, telling the soldier with the shield to advance past the other two groups. They were the first to meet the skeletons.

The shield did its job to deflect the attacks as they shattered the bones of the skeletons and began to destroy the force ahead of them. With each step, they closed the gap between them and the Evocator.

Howls erupted from the hounds when one of their own fell to the soldiers in the columns, and the hound nearest to Luke's column headed toward its fallen comrade.

Soldiers began to scream as the hound tore into one of them, leaving the others scattered on the ground.

"Go back and help the others!" Luke told the group to his right, and the group instantly went to help the other columns. He could see that Beatrix was holding her ground against the skeletons, and Marius was still in command of the soldiers, but the hounds weren't allowing them to get back into formation. It was chaos, and they were barely holding on. He couldn't tell how many soldiers were down, with all the skeletons mixed in the fighting.

The ground shook, and claws erupted from the dirt beside Luke's group. The head started pushing its way out. "To our right!"

Luke slashed down at the hound's face, slicing a large

gash into its skull. He continued to slash at it as they turned their shield to face its complete form.

Its claws ripped toward the shield, yanking it out of the soldier's hand and pulling him with it.

The soldier screamed as the hound pressed its clawed foot into his chest and stared at Luke and the other defenseless soldier.

Luke threw his hand behind him, pulled his ancile from its sheath, and faced down the hound. The soldier's screaming stopped, and the hound shoved the body aside, focusing intently on the two in front of it.

It all happened in slow motion. The soldier glanced over his shoulder to see where the other group of soldiers was, and Luke screamed, running toward the soldier to defend him. In only a matter of seconds, the soldier met his end at the hound's jaws. Luke had been too late, his blades missing the hound by inches.

The sound coming from the hound sounded like a chuckle. It was gloating over its kill. Now Luke could see the other group of soldiers behind the hound, but its eyes were only on him. It wasn't worried about what was behind it.

Luke needed the hound to change direction only for a moment. He screamed, flipping his right wrist. He flipped his ancile to have the long edge outward and lunged forward as the hound sped toward him. He slammed his left ancile into the dirt and moved back onto his leading leg, bringing his right ancile down to the right.

The hound, with its speed, narrowly avoided the ancile in the ground, and Luke's blade connected with the hound's side as its clawed paw hit him in the leg.

Luke spun head over heels and landed on his back, his blade ripped from his hands. The hound howled as it tried to remove the blade from its back.

Luke pushed himself off the ground, pulled the ancile out of the dirt, and rushed at the wounded hound. He sent his weapon downward, keeping his distance, and ended the hound's life.

The other soldiers finished off the skeletons, clearing the way to the Evocator.

Luke picked up his other blade and ran toward the Evocator to stop the incantation. The ground shook again, and Luke lost his footing as the structures grew farther out of the earth.

He braced himself as the earth shook; he could see the ancile blade in the Evocator's right hand. When the quake diminished, he closed the distance to the Evocator, who turned to face him. Bones shot out of the ground and formed a shield in front of his arm and in his right hand formed around the broken ancile to in the shape a coarse, curved blade. He waved his hands, and skeletons rushed toward the others. This fight was only going to be the two of them.

The laughter that rang out of his voice was hideous, and Luke had barely enough time to lift his blade to stop from being gutted.

Luke parried the blade with his left, and the shield connected against his arm, sending him back a step. The movement of the Evocator was that of the hound. It was hard to focus on his movements as he tried to stay alive. The small, shielded area of his ancile was barely enough to keep the blade away from his vital organs.

Luke hadn't kept track of his surroundings and tripped over a rock. The Evocator brought his blade toward Luke's chest, and Luke parried it to the side, kicking upward.

He caught the Evocator's leg, causing him to fall to one knee. The hood fell off the Evocator's face to reveal a man whose black curly hair bounced as he shook his head. Luke rolled to his left, the boned blade sticking into the dirt beside him.

Luke moved to his feet, lifted both blades in front of him, and charged. The Evocator was on his feet and raised his shield.

Taking a chance, Luke threw his fist right into the boned shield, allowing the short end of the blade and shield to absorb most of the impact.

The Evocator slammed his shield forward against the attack. Chips of bone flew from the shield as it threw Luke's arm out wide and knocked his blade out of his hand. Luke's forward momentum carried him right into the Evocator, who went down with him.

He dropped his other blade when they connected. Shaking himself off the ground, he found the bone blade close to him.

Lifting the blade, he rushed the weaponless Evocator. Blue fire erupted in the Evocator's hand, and a spear of bone appeared in the air, aimed right at Luke.

The blade sunk into the Evocator's skin; instantly the fire died in the Evocator's hands. The bone spear dropped to the dirt, and the Evocator fell to his knees, looking dazed at what had happened. Then he gazed at Luke and spoke. "What have you done?"

Bones fell from the blade to reveal the broken ancile beneath, and blue fire enveloped the Evocator.

The clouds dispersed into the air, revealing the blue sky once more. That's when Luke saw the Evocator stand up, pulling the blade out, and looked directly at him. Blue fire filled his eyes, the bones against his body shifted to make a rattling sound, and the skull on his shoulder erupted with burning red eyes.

"I feel like I've been trapped within that cursed

blade for ages," the man spoke.

Luke recognized the voice immediately. It didn't have the raspy voice of the shade, but it was distinct enough for him to identify who it was. "Rufus."

Chapter 12: For the Realm

Circular rings of stone stood above the earth's surface, forming the top of towers that had once stood watch over Vallis Ossa. Slits ran through the exterior of the exposed building, but it only reached the height of a horse above the surface.

Rufus stood before the towers, his eyes upon Luke. With the wave of his hand, Rufus had all the skeletons depart the conflict and stand in line behind him. The hound sprinted away and settled beside Rufus.

The soldiers formed up, preparing for the conflict. Luke waved his column to fall in line with Beatrix and Marius, then started to move. The hound growled, baring its menacing teeth.

"Now that isn't very astute of you," Rufus said. "The hound would like it if you stayed where you are. All of you." Rufus pointed to soldiers behind Luke.

Luke felt very close to Rufus and the hound. He glanced back and could see the worry on the faces of Marius and Beatrix. The soldiers anxiously stood, awaiting orders.

Rufus continued. "This body will have to do for now. I do hope that we can come to an agreement that is acceptable to us all."

"We brought you to Rubrum Castellum as you

requested," Luke said. "Now keep your end of the deal."

"There was no such deal, only that we would continue our agreement," Rufus sneered at Luke. "Shall we continue?"

"Luke, what are you doing?" Marius called from behind him.

Luke wished he had been able to tell the others about the cursed blade and Rufus. Now it was too late to try and fill them in and make any sort of plan.

"He knows how to save Lady Aurelia!" Luke yelled back to the others.

A commotion rose throughout the troops as they murmured to one another. It died down a moment later, and Marius said, "Don't make a deal with him. Whatever Aurelia did, she made that choice for the realm."

"This deal doesn't concern you, Marius," Rufus said.

"I have never met you. How is it that you know of me?" Marius called to him.

Rufus responded smugly, "I know a great deal about all of you. General Marius Wilhelm, Lady Beatrix Scorpio, and Luke Valor. Each of you were part of the memories I shared with Lady Aurelia, fragmented memories, but with time on my hands, I was able to put them together. Now if you please, let me converse with

Luke privately on this matter."

Marius started to speak, but Luke knew what he would ask and spoke first. "It's Rufus, the Evocator Aurelia went after."

Again the commotion started and died down. Marius must have silenced them, but he heard Beatrix's voice. "Luke, whatever he promised you is a lie. Aurelia's gone. We can't allow this to continue."

The hound growled, and the skeletons stepped forward. Luke turned toward the soldiers and signed to them, "*We have to try.*"

They stopped, and Luke could feel the hound breathing behind him. He signed once more, "*Let me try.*" Then he turned to face the hound and Rufus once more. "How do we know that Lady Aurelia is alive and well?"

Rufus's hand was covered in blue fire, and three spears of bone floated high above his head. "There is an easy way to show her to you—I am a bit antsy, you see. Being locked up in that blade for years does that to one's mental state." The spears shifted forward in the sky. "Now if you'd please return back to your original positions, we'll continue."

Luke turned back to Marius and Beatrix and signed, "*Step back, and I'll signal to you when I'm ready.*"

"It would be greatly appreciated if you'd speak the

words you're telling your soldiers," Rufus said, the spears continuing their advance.

"Step back. I'm fine," Luke said out loud and then turned back toward Rufus. "Please continue."

Moments passed before Rufus let the spears fall to the ground, and the hound resumed its position by his side.

"Now where were we? Ah yes. Lady Aurelia is safe beneath these ruins, alive and breathing," Rufus said, his voice filled with venom. "That vile woman took everything from me, all in the name of your pathetic realm."

Luke could tell Rufus hated Aurelia from those words. Rufus would never let him walk away alive. "Are you saying that she is alive underground?"

Rufus filled his hand with the bluish fire once more, and an image shimmered to the side of him. A woman hovered above the ground, hunched forward with a crystal protruding from her chest, her hands pressed tightly against the crystal. She wore the Ancilian armor, her hair hung about her face, and only the radiant blue colors streamed from the image.

"Her body rests suspended in time at the moment of her death." Rufus spun the image around slowly to show all aspects of her form.

Luke could only see that she was alive, spinning in

the air before him. He could see Aurelia, and he needed to know how to save her. "How do we get to her? How far down is she?"

"Far," Rufus said and then closed his fist. The image disappeared. "She holds my crystallum in her hands, and only those who love and hold her dear to their hearts may reach her. That is why you are here. That is why we had to come together to this place."

"Then show me how to reach her." Luke stood defiantly before the hound and Rufus.

"Don't believe him," Marius said. "I've seen magic like this before. It isn't real."

"Luke, we have to get out of here," Beatrix called after him.

It was all noise now, meaningless words. Maybe they were too far to see Aurelia in the image. It was her. That's all that mattered right now. "Let's make a deal," Luke said.

"Now that is courage," Rufus said. "The city has fallen far beneath the earth, and we've only started to bring it back from beneath. When linked with my Evocator, we had risen the city to only where you see it now, and with you dispatching him, I am feeling both grateful and vengeful." He paused. "Without my staff, my power is only half of what it was, and it will be impossible for me to continue my work here—which brings us to our arrangement."

The hound stepped forward, its growls intensifying. Luke could hear footsteps from behind him.

"There is no need for this." It was Marius. "The realm doesn't do business with your kind, and I cannot allow this to continue."

"If my Evocator didn't scare you, then you surely are mistaken, Marius." Rufus snapped his fingers with a blue flame, and the ground shook. "Yes, my power is limited without my staff, but it does exceed that of my apprentices."

Two more daemon hounds crawled from beneath the surface, while more skeletons pulled themselves together, forming behind the soldiers in the back. "From the look in your eyes, you know these hounds. Something from your past perhaps, a reminder of all those you lost? I would hate to see you sacrifice the lives of so many because of your pride."

Marius stopped feet away from Luke and grumbled, "Heh, don't let me stop you now."

Luke wanted to tell Marius off before he ruined everything. He had to hold his own tongue, and now they were in worse trouble than before.

"Now where were we? Ah yes. My staff. Without it, there is no way to reach Aurelia." Rufus lifted his hand, displaying another figure. A man just below Luke's height, with curly hair, a sharp chin with slanted cheekbones, and a lean frame stood spinning in the air. He shifted from one image to another, one looking behind him with fear in his eyes as he held a staff of bone in his hand, and then he appeared to be running away from the image, cloak billowing behind him.

"Felix," Luke said.

"Ah, so you know him?" Rufus asked.

Marius chimed in, "Yes, we know him." Luke caught on that he didn't want to give any details to Rufus.

"This is the man who has my staff, and without it, Aurelia will remain frozen in time," Rufus said.

"Felix is…" Luke started.

"We'll find him," Marius said. "Are you sure that he has the staff in his possession?"

Rufus nodded.

"Then we'll return with Felix and the staff," Marius said. His hand pressed down firmly on Luke's shoulder and pulled him back a step.

"How naive do you believe me to be?" Rufus snapped. The hounds and the skeletons began to march forward. "Felix has been missing for years. My apprentices haven't been able to locate him and if they had, they went missing." Rufus's eyes began to glow blue. "Your lies are unbecoming of you, Marius."

Luke could see the forces move toward them. It was

only a matter of seconds. "We'll find him and retrieve your staff. You have my word."

Everything stopped. "How are you to succeed where others haven't? Where would you go first, and why should I believe you?"

Luke had thought of everything over and over for the past three years. He had to keep going, and he knew where Felix had last been seen. "Lady Aurelia has been in my thoughts for the last three years, and now that we are this close to bringing her home, I'm not going to give up now. The last we heard of Felix was at Cymatilis Port. That's where we'll look for him first."

It was quiet for a moment before Rufus spoke. "Now those are words of truth." He flicked his hand, blue fire in its wake. Bones shook through the dirt and crafted themselves into a skeletal horse. "Felix has found a way to hide the staff from my sight. Either way, one of us will recover the staff and return here. I do hope that we meet again—that is, if you survive." Rufus lifted himself upon the skeletal horse, and the hounds surrounded him. Then he took off, heading southwest toward the port. Two hounds followed behind him, along with a few skeletons. One of the hounds and a handful of skeletons stayed behind to cover his escape.

"For the realm!" Marius yelled as he moved to the side, smashing a skeleton to pieces, and the soldiers charged forward.

"Luke!" Beatrix screamed as the hound bounded for Luke, weaponless and alone.

Chapter 13: Aftermath

The hound changed direction and followed after Rufus. The soldiers cleared the field of the last of the Inmortuae and began counting their losses. They had gone in fighting with the strength of twenty-eight soldiers, and now they were down to twenty soldiers spread between the columns, not including the wounded.

The brilliantly red-orange sun dipped beyond the horizon in the west. The tranquil, gorgeous moment of the descending sun was not enjoyed by the Ancilian soldiers. There had been too much loss to enjoy such a view.

They set up camp outside the ruins, ready for combat, and the officers went from the soldiers to converse with one another.

"If my honor didn't bind me to protect you, I would have let you rot in the afterlife!" Marius growled at Luke. "The whole realm is now that risk because of your actions. I should have followed my gut and halted the mission before it began!"

"It isn't his fault," Beatrix stepped in. "There was no way he knew this would happen—none of us did. We now know more than we did, and that's what the mission was about."

"Heh. The mission," Marius grumbled.

Luke listened to Marius groan about their losses, and he shared the pain of his own soldiers. It wasn't easy to lose them. He blamed himself, and it wasn't helping that Marius was accusing him. "You told me to not take the honor of the fallen and that they gave their lives to the realm. That is why we are here, devoting ourselves to the realm in search of Lady Aurelia."

"Using my words against me?" Marius stepped toward Luke. "How many more soldiers have to die before you give up this search for her? How many Evocators have you come across in your lifetime? You believed a traitor to the realm? A man who devoted his entire existence to destroying Arcem Regni!" He shoved Luke's chest. "Aurelia did her job. She sacrificed her life to destroy that madman, and you made a deal with him. What would she think of you now?"

Luke was sick of Marius pushing him around. He gripped the front of Marius's chest piece, shoving him backward. "I'm tired of you treating me like I am a nobody, like everyone has been tolerating me because I was Nero's son and only a burden to the realm."

Beatrix tried to stop the nonsense but could not prevent it from happening.

Marius shoved Luke's hands off, and Luke threw a punch at Marius. Marius moved away from the fist, gripped it, and pulled Luke off his feet. He fell to his knees and scrambled up to his feet. Marius kicked him in the side, and he fell to the ground, out of breath.

"The realm tolerates you because of your deeds, but your obsession with Lady Aurelia has gone on long enough," Marius said. "The mission is over. We're to regroup with the reinforcements and then head back to Arcem Regni; preparations will be made for how we'll deal with Rufus and his followers. No thanks to you."

Beatrix cleared her throat, but Marius had already walked away.

She reached down and helped Luke back to his feet as he fought to catch his breath. "I'm sorry."

"Don't apologize; it's very unbecoming of the future lord of the realm," she said as she brushed the dust off his chest. "The only exception is when you're apologizing to me, but for this situation, it wasn't your fault."

"It was," Luke said. "I should have told you that Rufus's soul was trapped in her blade. That's why I am apologizing, for not telling you the whole truth."

Beatrix stood quietly.

"I know that you're upset with me, but the timing was never right. When you first described the mission and told me that we'd be investigating the ruins, I didn't want to stop it from going through. That's why I kept my mouth shut, even while we were heading out in the field. Wasn't right then."

"If his soul was trapped in the blade, then why was he standing right there in front of us?" Beatrix went right to the point.

Luke told her what had happened during the conflict. The blade came in contact with the Evocator, and then Rufus was there.

Beatrix paced back and forth. "This is bad. Really bad. Marius has it out for you and has already called off the mission. And knowing my mother's state, she won't let me protect you anymore."

"You need to let me go," Luke pleaded. "I need to go to Port Cymatilis and see if Felix is still alive. I have to."

Beatrix stopped and stared at him. "You don't think it's a trick? You believe that my sister is still alive and what he showed us was real?"

"Yes."

"When I saw her there, I wanted to believe it. But I can't allow myself to believe the words of a traitor; I would lose the faith of the realm," Beatrix said.

"Then don't. Let me go this one alone, and when I return back to Arcem Regni, it will either be as a deserter or the hero who brought Aurelia home." Luke gripped Beatrix's hand. "My life is expendable, whereas you are not. The realm needs your strength and leadership, while I've only been a burden people carried around."

"You aren't a burden to me." Beatrix squeezed his hand.

"I don't know how I would have made it through all these years without you believing in me," Luke said.

"I could say the same to you." Beatrix smiled.

"Heh." They hadn't heard Marius approaching. "I hate to interrupt whatever this is. Everyone is ready back at camp for us to brief them. Would hate for us to not show a unified front after all we've been through."

Beatrix dropped Luke's hand. "About that unified front…"

Beatrix let Marius know that she was still in charge of this mission, and it wasn't over. They were to send a rider back to Arcem Regni and inform Lady Ursus of the dire situation surrounding Rufus. They were continuing onward to Cymatilis Port. Additional reinforcements would secure the locations in the realm. Rubrum Castellum, Cymatilis Port, and the roads would be reinforced with more soldiers.

Marius disapproved, but Beatrix was relentless about her decision. They were to continue their march tomorrow southwest toward Cymatilis Port.

Beatrix walked back toward the camp, leaving Marius and Luke behind.

"Heh. What a lady of the realm, and I don't see what she sees in you," Marius grumbled to Luke. He had lost the argument.

"Neither do I," Luke agreed.

Chapter 14: Port of Cymatilis

Southwest of the ruins was the port of Cymatilis. Known for catering to thousands of ships per year, it served as a hub for import, warehousing, and the distribution of resources that ensured the realm's stability.

The rivers and canals led into the great ocean upon which the port was built. A diamond-shaped structure surrounded the middle of the port, providing access for smaller boats and ships to deliver their goods to the market. A causeway led out to the main docks of the port, where the larger vessels set anchor and sent their goods inward on smaller boats. The stone structure surrounded the bowl, ending with a large opening out to sea. Along the walls stood towers distanced to protect and guard the port from invaders. Outside the port stood a lighthouse to guide the ships looking for the port.

Stone buildings with their slated clay-tiled rooftops lined the port's walls, with very few buildings close to the diamond-shaped center. There, near the center, were tents where merchants and traders conducted their business.

On the road, officers and their columns looked down upon the port with awe and wonder of the beautiful, reflective surface of the water that carried the ships gently across its calm waters.

They had passed wagons of goods heading toward the city of Arcem Regni, along with the hired guards to protect them. The guards had warned them that there could be trouble along the roads before they continued on their way.

There was no sign of Rufus or the others along their journey to the port. The tracks had vanished miles away from the ruins. They had kept their eyes open, awaiting an ambush to occur; luckily they made it with no trouble at all.

Luke looked down at the port. Over a year ago, they had gone looking for Felix and found only his armor as a clue, nothing else. Eventually, it had become a dead end, and now they were back looking for him.

Beatrix and Marius moved away from their columns and pulled Luke aside for a quiet discussion before entering the port.

"The mission is still to find Lady Aurelia or clues about her survival," Beatrix said. "If Felix is alive, he'll be able to help us."

"He is a deserter and left the lady alone to die. If he knows what's good for him, he won't come quietly," Marius said.

Luke had thought long and hard about what they

would do when they found Felix. "Our best chance is to get him to tell us where the staff is and work with him. If we go in there looking to arrest him as a deserter, he'll likely run or continue to hide."

"Agreed," Beatrix stated.

"Heh. Just don't go making a deal with him that the realm won't back," Marius said. "He deserted the lady in her time of need, and it's probably the reason he's been hiding out all this time."

"We can't go in marching around legions in front of the crowds. It's best if we try to separate into groups and go looking for him," Luke suggested; "we can gather what information we can and cover more ground this way."

"We'll separate into groups of three and return to the gates at dusk to report," Beatrix stated. "Take two soldiers from each column—"

"Milady, you're staying at the gates," Marius interrupted.

Beatrix scowled. "General Wilhelm, I am going out in search of this deserter to get the answers we need. Having me wait at the gates is a waste of time."

"Heh. Then I'm going with you, and we're bringing additional soldiers with us, and that's final," Marius responded.

"Fine," Beatrix settled.

They dissolved their meeting and returned to their columns as they entered the gates. From there, they broke into separated groups; each was to report back at dusk, and their search began.

Luke took two soldiers from his column and headed southwest through the streets of Cymatilis, while the others headed southeast.

The buildings were roughly carved stone layered atop one another and intertwined with cement. Clay tiles on the rooftops allowed very little shade for the streets below.

Luke and the soldiers asked bystanders if they knew the name Felix Rius, a legion officer who had settled in the port in the last three years or so. Most of the responses were a hard no. Others had recently moved to the port and were used to soldiers coming and going, but no one knew the name.

They continued down the streets and entered the marketplace. The streets were busy with people going from tent to tent searching for goods. Pushing past people, they continued to ask about any sightings of a man with curly red hair with sharp features who lived at port or was seen recently. The answers were becoming the same, a resounding no.

The sun started moving toward dusk, and they had nothing to report.

"Excuse me." A young woman approached them and grabbed on to Luke's arm. "Are you looking for a curly-haired man?"

Luke looked down to find a woman shorter than him wearing a cloak, which was drawn close to her face. Her hair slid through the hood, making it hard to make out her features. "Yes, we are," he replied.

"You're looking for Xaine. He owns the buildings near the water's edge." She pointed further down the road to one of the more significant buildings settled right before the wall circled out into the ocean. "There."

Then she took off running. Luke tried to follow her but lost her in the crowd. They moved toward the building and settled two houses down from it. It was decorated with banners, and guards were posted at the entrance, dressed in robes that covered them to their boots. Their hoods had slits that allowed them to breathe and see through. Clothing like that would cause anyone to overheat in this springtime weather. The constantly evaporating ocean water increased the temperature and humidity in the surrounding area.

"Don't like the look of those guards, and who knows what or who is in the building," Luke said to the soldiers with him. "One of you go back and inform the others that we need to check this place out. We'll keep watch in case someone decides to make a run for it."

"On it," One of the soldiers replied and turned to leave. "Um, sir."

Luke turned back and found four of the full-robed garbed guards standing behind them, and a man stepped between them. He wore a cloak with the hood on, and Luke could see the red curly hair and a sharp chin beneath.

"Been a while, Valor. I hear you've been looking for me," the man spoke. "Let's take this back to my place."

Chapter 15: Xaine Rutilus

Luke and the soldiers drew their weapons as the man in the hood spoke. They had been on edge since their previous encounters and weren't going to allow anything to happen again.

The man lifted his hands. "Lower your weapons. As a gesture of goodwill, we will allow one of your soldiers to go and get the others. Try and not bring the whole legion; I have a reputation to uphold."

Luke moved between his soldiers. "I don't trust you."

"And you shouldn't." A smile could be seen under the hood. "But the discussion we're about to have should be taken inside, where prying ears aren't nearby. Allow me to show you that I mean no harm." The guards surrounding the man moved away and headed for the building. "Better?"

Luke watched until they disappeared past the guards and into the building and then slid his blades away. He looked around the building and saw a place that looked out over the ocean. "While one of my soldiers goes and retrieves the others, let's have our discussion on that wall. My soldier will stand guard."

"Let's continue." The man walked past Luke and wandered to the wall overlooking the ocean.

"Go find Beatrix and Marius. Tell them that I believe

we've found Felix, and I need them here now," Luke told the soldier, and he left to find the others. "Call for me if you see any sign of trouble, anything at all. Don't hesitate for anything suspicious. We can't get caught flat footed again." The remaining soldier nodded, and they made their way to the wall.

The ocean was beautifully calm, with the glowing sun, a half circle in the orange-red sky, illuminated a quivering path across the water.

"Are you going to drop the hood to reveal who you truly are?" Luke asked the man once he stood beside him.

"You know who I am," the man spoke.

"Fel…"

"The man who went by that name died a long time ago—three years, to be exact. My name is Xaine Rutilus, and I already know who you are, Luke Valor," the man said.

After years, they finally found someone who had been there at the end with Aurelia. Anger rose up in Luke, making him want to lash out and take Felix/Xaine down and get the answers he wanted, but he held back. Marius would probably do that, and Luke wanted answers before that happened.

"Why didn't you return back to Arcem Regni and report?" Luke asked.

"Do you see the sunset—the way it moves down beyond the endless ocean from here?" Xaine asked. Luke had no idea what that had to do with anything, but Xaine continued without waiting for a reply. "Feels final when it drops off the face of the realm, until the next morning where it rises from the east once again."

He then turned toward Luke, dropping his hood, revealing the red curls underneath that grew along the sides, reaching his shoulders but trimmed back behind the ears. "I thought about returning back to Arcem Regni, but I knew it would be over for me, with an ending where I'd never see the sunrise again."

"No one ever returned home. We had no answers or clues about what happened back at Rubrum Castellum," Luke said. "Lady Aurelia never returned home, but peace returned to the realm. Now here you are, three years later."

"If I returned home, it wouldn't be as a hero but as a coward. Alone, without answers to her parents and to the realm." Xaine raised his hands in the air. "The sole survivor has returned."

Luke knew exactly how that would look to the realm, that Xaine had something to do with the disappearance of Lady Aurelia, but not returning at all was even more suspicious. "At least we'd have answers about how you had survived when others didn't, about what really happened at Rubrum Castellum—but instead you decided on self-preservation."

"Wouldn't you?"

"No. I've been mourning, waiting for answers for the last three years while you lived your life out here." Luke was getting more upset with each part of their conversation. Time was fleeting before the others would arrive. "Tell me what happened back at Rubrum Castellum."

"If you insist," Xaine said, looking at the ocean instead of Luke as he spoke. "When we found the city, it was overrun with Daemons and Inmortuae. Our losses were great. We fought our way into the city, where we reached the dome where the ritual was taking place."

"What ritual?"

"Let me finish before you ask questions," Xaine snapped. "We found the Evocator in the middle of a ritual to open a way into the realm for the Daemon, and we saw countless Daemon awaiting entrance." Xaine shook his head. "Aurelia wouldn't stop or turn back; she kept talking about 'for the realm' nonsense and ended up fighting her way in. Lesser Daemons were allowed passage through the doorway, while others could only gaze in. Eventually more and more soldiers fell at the hands of the Daemons and Inmortuae before Aurelia stopped the ritual, ending her life."

"She died?" Luke asked, remembering the image Rufus had shown him.

"Yes, the Evocator struck her down and turned for me after she had closed the doorway. That's when the earthquakes started, and the buildings began to sink into the ground. I fought my way out with a handful of soldiers but eventually was the only one who made it out alive."

"You're the only one who survived?" Luke asked. There had to be others if he had made it out.

"Yes, the whole city was swallowed up into the earth, and when I looked for survivors, there were none," Xaine said. "I looked for ways into the city and decided that I had better return home, but that's when it dawned on me that being the sole survivor wouldn't work out when I returned. That's when I came here and decided to make a new life for myself."

Things weren't adding up for Luke. The clues leading to his armor being here matched, but it felt wrong. "Why couldn't we find you when we came looking for you here years ago?"

"I wasn't foolish enough to hide anywhere in the realm where Marius could find me. That man is relentless. I waited until things calmed down, with the occasional visit to the port for supplies."

It covered for that fact that they hadn't found him,

but Felix/Xaine hadn't been the best soldier in the field, and him ending up as the sole survivor was hard to believe. Luke glanced back at the soldier to see if anyone else had approached, but there was nothing. Time for more questions.

"We found Rubrum Castellum in ruins years ago, with no survivors or fallen. The city had vanished, but we never thought to look beneath the surface," Luke said. "For years, more and more gave up hope of finding Aurelia until a clue arrived at my home."

After the long pause, Xaine asked, "What clue?"

"Her ancile, broken," Luke said, letting it be at that.

"That's why you are here? Looking for answers because of her ancile? After everything had calmed down, you're here because of that? What ill fate on my part, but I'm not going back a prisoner of war or deserter. I'll fight if that's why you're here."

Luke wondered how much he should tell him about Rufus. Xaine had left out the essential details of him hightailing it out of the city with the staff; either Rufus was lying or Xaine was. He needed to know which one.

"The ancile was the beginning; it allowed us to investigate Rubrum Castellum one last time before we would let the past be," Luke said, wanting to know if he'd reveal anything else. "That's when we found another clue that led us to you."

Xaine shifted anxiously, waiting for Luke to continue with what they found, but Luke grew silent, deciding to let him become restless.

"Officer Valor," The soldier called. Luke glanced back and saw two of Xaine's guards step up beside the soldier, but they made no move against him.

"What are your guards doing?" Luke asked.

"Give me a moment." Xaine turned and waved them off, and they complied with his command. "Nervous habit. What clue led you to me?"

Nervous habit? Luke thought. What was that all about? "We encountered an Evocator rising the city from the ground, and it worked," he said, conveniently leaving out the part where they'd stopped him.

Xaine's face gave away that he knew something. "What did you find in the city?"

"Nothing."

"Aurelia wasn't there?" Xaine let that slip.

"Why would she be there? If she died during that encounter, her body would have decomposed."

"Did you find her remains and her armor? You knew what she was wearing when she left," Xaine spoke coldly to him.

Luke was sick of going around in circles with Xaine. "What are you not telling me?"

"Nothing. You're not telling me how that led you to

find me."

Luke had been waiting for the others to get there, but they were taking quite a bit of time to arrive, and he was done asking questions. He needed to get answers.

"Enough with the games—the Evocator we engaged with said you took something that belonged to him, and he wants it back."

That got a reaction out of Xaine, who pulled his hood over his head and stepped away from Luke.

"You brought him here!" Xaine screamed. Blue shades of fire danced beneath the hood.

"Soldier!" Luke called. Turning, he saw the soldier gone from his post and found Beatrix, Marius, and two soldiers surrounded by Inmortuae. Walking up the wall was a man with his hair slicked back on his head.

"My apprentice doesn't seem too happy to see me."

Chapter 16: Escaping Cymatilis

Luke had felt that there was something off about Xaine, and seeing the blue orbs underneath the hood, it all started to make sense now. Had he genuinely been working for Rufus the entire time? "Apprentice?" Luke asked, looking back to Xaine, who now held blue fire in his hands.

"You shouldn't be here. You're dead. I saw it with my own eyes," Xaine spoke.

"Thank Valor over here, without him I'd probably still be trapped," Rufus said, continuing his approach up to the wall. "Magnificent work shielding yourself and my staff from my sight. The search would have been rather tedious without our friends here."

There was a sound coming from wall overlooking the ocean, scraping against stone. Luke knew of only one thing they had faced in the last couple of days that it could be, and he was too close to it for comfort. "Let them go, and you can have him." He turned toward Xaine, hoping that he hadn't forgotten all his training, and signed with his back to Rufus, "*Go with it. Hound. Wall. Need to run.*" He rushed toward Xaine and slid his ancile under his chin. "Without him, you'll never find your staff."

Rufus lifted his hands. The scraping and Inmortuae

stopped where they were. "Do you remember our first encounter, Luke? I do not fear you. I think I've decided you're a liability, and I should take other precautions for our arrangement."

Beatrix screamed as a skeleton pulled her hair and started dragging her away.

Marius shouted and was quickly knocked to his knees by the skeletons around him. His face showed more annoyance than pain.

"Where did you hide the staff?" Luke quickly asked Xaine. His eyes were intently focused on Beatrix being hauled away. "Where is it!" Luke shoved Xaine toward Rufus, hoping for a miracle as he ran forward to get to Marius and Beatrix.

A howl broke through the night, and the hound bounded atop the wall behind him. Xaine's hooded guardsmen leaped from the top of the building. More guards rushed out from the alleyways and began fighting the Inmortuae that surrounded Marius and the soldiers.

Relieved, Luke rushed toward the skeleton hauling Beatrix and found she had freed herself, leaving a pile of bones in her wake.

"We need to get out of here now!" Luke continued to run toward Beatrix as Marius followed suit. The hooded guards and Inmortuae were heavily engaged with one another. Blue streaks flew along the wall as Rufus and Xaine continued their fight. However, the hound had set its sight on Luke and them.

"Marius, get Beatrix back to the safety of the legions while we deal with this hound," Luke said as they ran through the streets. People began to scream as they saw the battle raging by the water's edge and ran for safety. "There are going to be a lot more causalities if we try to outrun that thing."

"That's your plan?" Marius asked.

"Got a better one?"

"Stop, both of you, and let's take that thing down!" Beatrix said as she stopped, turning to face the hound, her weapon in hand.

The soldiers, Marius, and Luke skidded to a stop and turned to face the hound as well. It slowed its approach, focused intently on Luke and them. A howl burst from its throat, and it charged Beatrix. Luke lifted his ancilia, crossing them in front of his body, and leaped in front of her.

The hound stopped abruptly before hitting his ancilia full force and shook its head.

"Do you have a death wish?!" Xaine appeared behind the hound, his hand glowing brightly. "We need to get to the canals. Follow my guards; I'll deal with this."

Luke looked up, opening his eyes. He hadn't thought about what would happen when the hound hit him. He had just hoped it would work.

"Go!" Xaine yelled as a few of his guards appeared in the shadows. He motioned them forward down the street.

They followed and could see the hound turn and charge toward Rufus and his Inmortuae. Luke guessed that Xaine had done something to the hound to cause it to switch targets.

They ran into more Inmortuae hiding in the shadows and quickly dispatched them. Luke slammed his fist into the skull of one of the skeletons and continued to move forward with the others.

Marius took out his annoyance on a few of the skeletons, parrying aside their weapons and breaking their bones, sending them flying into the marketplace. Bystanders continued to scream.

They followed the guards into an alley and right into a dead end.

"We're trapped," Marius said. "We should have taken our chances with the hound."

"Let's go back." Luke turned back the way they had come.

The guards grunted and started lifting a stone from the wall. The rock had to have weighed a couple hundred pounds, and they were moving it easily together.

A few moments went by before the stone was moved, and they waved them in.

"What if it's a trap?" Marius said. "We should head back to the legions instead of going into that tunnel."

"Do we have a choice?" Beatrix questioned. "These guards work for Xaine, and he told us to follow them here."

"Trust the deserter. I am really getting too old for this," Marius said. "The next mission I go on, I'm leaving both of you at home."

Xaine came huffing around the corner, his hood had fallen back, and he looked irritated. "Get in; what are you doing sitting out here. Go, go!" Everyone watched as he pushed past and went into the tunnel, lighting the darkness with his hands. "Close it. They can either join me or stay out there and die."

The guards started to push the stone back into place. They looked at each other, and Beatrix slipped inside before Marius could grab her arm. He grunted and followed her, as did Luke and the other soldiers.

The stone was placed back into place, and Xaine ordered them to be quiet and follow him. They moved down the tunnel and heard commotion back outside in the alleyway. Soon, the sounds drifted farther behind them.

As they continued down the tunnel, they heard the sound of water flowing beside them and the overwhelming smell of it. It was horrid. Plugging and covering their noses any way they could, they continued onward. The walkway was all that stood between them and the murky water below, and it was big enough for two people to stand side by side without fear of falling into the water below.

Farther down, they could see very little light illuminating the end of the tunnel. Xaine lifted his hand for them to stop before progressing any farther.

"What happened back there?" Luke whispered to Xaine. "That hound turned on Rufus—did you do that?"

"Yes," Xaine said, letting the light from his hands fade away. "Took quite a bit out of me to do that, but his hold isn't what it used to be."

"Where are we going?!" Marius shouted, his voice echoing through the tunnel. He shoved Xaine up against the wall. "Good to see you again. Now if you'd be so kind as to tell me what's going on around here before I break that pretty smile of yours."

Xaine lifted his hands. "Marius, keep your voice down until everything calms down. I'll tell you what I know."

"Heh. Good." Marius released him and stepped in front of Xaine, blocking his escape.

Xaine filled Marius in with the same information he had told Luke on the wall—how he had gone into hiding for a time, changed his name, and everything that had happened back at Rubrum Castellum. Luke filled in where he could, while Beatrix and Marius listened intently.

Luke knew there were still questions he hadn't gotten the answers to. "What about the staff? Rufus showed an image of you running away with it. Do you have it?"

Xaine gazed down without answering.

Marius was there again in a heartbeat, lifting him against the wall. "I don't care how strong you think you are—tell us the truth!"

"Yes, I took it and ran," Xaine admitted. "I saw an opportunity and took the staff from him and ran for it."

"Then it's true. You did take it and run. Now what about my sister? What really happened to her?" Beatrix joined in on the conversation.

The shadowed form of Xaine in the darkness lowered his head and began to tell them what really happened.

Aurelia had been knocked aside by Rufus during his ritual, only to recover and take his crystallum before he completed it. The Daemons howled in frustration as the gate closed between their worlds, and Rufus tried to stop her. She stepped into the ritual circle and slammed her ancile into his chest. Aurelia couldn't prevent the crystallum from slowly entering her chest. A sphere of blue surrounded her body, and Rufus collapsed. Xaine —Felix at the time—took the opportunity to take his staff, and when he saw no hope for Aurelia, he sprinted for the exit, urging all to follow him. They fought through the Daemons, and Felix became become trapped within the falling city without a way out.

He searched for a way out and eventually found an exit leading to a hidden cave within the Vallis Ossa. There he stayed until the rumbling stopped, before working his way around the valley to the top of the mountain, where he found that Rubrum Castellum had disappeared entirely beneath the surface. That's when Xaine went to the port, leaving behind his armor and name, taking supplies back to the hidden cave where he stayed until things calmed down. Then he made his home in the Port of Cymatilis until they found him.

Marius was quite upset that he had deserted Aurelia and never returned home despite the consequences he would face. Beatrix tried to calm him down the best she could.

Luke contemplated the new information. Aurelia was stuck with that crystallum in her chest, in the sphere Rufus had shown them. "Ahem," he cleared his throat, stopping the others from continuing their arguing about desertion and their laws. "Rufus said that we can still save her. Everything he told us up to now has been true. Could he be telling us the truth about saving her too?"

"There is always truth before the lies settle in," Marius said. "When you confirm the truths, you rush into the lies at full speed, believing in those too."

"Yes," Luke concurred. "He wants the staff and is going back after his crystallum. If he retrieves that without us being there to stop him, he'll kill her."

"He needs the staff and doesn't have it. Felix does," Beatrix said. "Without it, he can't continue."

Luke went over the conversation he had with Rufus and remembered another step. "He needs one of us."

All heads turned toward Luke in the darkness.

"What do you mean by that?" Beatrix asked.

Luke told them about his first discussion with the shade of Rufus. How he had mentioned that if Luke wasn't willing to do it, he would go after another who held Aurelia dear to their heart or loved her, and that he'd mentioned Beatrix by name. That's why Beatrix had been dragged away from the others. He needed Luke or Beatrix for something.

"More reason for us to return back to Arcem Regni and bring the full force of the Ancilian army down upon Rufus," Marius said.

"Not before we get the staff. Once we have that, we can return home," Luke said, "Xaine, you need to give us the staff."

"No. I'm not going back now. I've already been called a traitor and a deserter by him." Xaine pointed at Marius. "Not going back to be put in chains for the rest of my life; I like the one I have."

Marius cracked his knuckles. "I don't think we were giving you the choice."

"Felix...Xaine, whoever you are only matters now. You're working with the realm to return Lady Aurelia safely home, and I believe that the future lady of the realm will find a way to excuse these accusations," Beatrix pleaded. "You've helped us escape and can continue to aid us in bringing her home. How does that sound?"

Xaine sat there in silence, mulling it over for a few minutes. "I want to hear Marius say it."

"Say what? Thank you?" Marius spoke.

"That you will drop the accusations," Xaine said. "Then I'll agree to helping you retrieve the staff."

Marius grumbled and turned around. Luke reached over and whispered in his ear, "It's now time for you to let this become a part of your past. Time to move forward with peace and hope for the future."

Marius turned and brought his face close to Luke's. "I don't think I like you very much." Then he faced Xaine. "Agreed. The charges against you will be dropped. Doesn't mean new ones can't be made."

"What do you mean by that?" Xaine asked.

"I know what you are, and I'm not quite sure how the realm is going to take having an Evocator on our side," Marius responded.

"Won't be the first time the Ancilians have worked with monsters," Xaine laughed. "I'm in."

"Finally, can we please get out of these tunnels? The smell is really getting to me," Beatrix said, moving forward toward the light.

"Not quite yet. It's best if we waited until morning," Xaine replied. "We don't want to get caught outside at night with Rufus around, and right now he's chasing my guards around in the hopes of finding us."

Beatrix sighed. Luke agreed that the smell was horrid, but they would have to make the best of it. Then Xaine told them that they needed to head to the hidden cave within Vallis Ossa to retrieve the staff.

Luke found his way over beside Beatrix, and they put their backs against each other and leaned against the wall. "Not the most romantic place to be," Luke said to her. "I think the next time we decide to take a stroll at night, let's avoid places like this."

She laughed. "Not sure I'd count this as any sort of outing. It's not just the two of us and if you ever took me to a place like this, I'd never forgive you."

"I distinctly remember following you into these tunnels. Remember that?" Luke reminded her.

"Making it my fault? You better remember who vouched for this mission in the first place," she chided him playfully. "If we were to keep score, this mission has put you into the negative."

They laughed, and it felt good to enjoy each other's company, although the foul odor kept wafting up from the water and into their nostrils no matter how hard they tried to avoid it.

"Do you think she's still alive?" Luke asked.

Beatrix was silent for a moment. "I believe she is. I do wonder how all of this will end; that's the hardest part for me. It's been three years, and everything has changed. It won't be the same world she was used to."

"She has us, and hopefully that's enough," Luke said.

"Yeah." Beatrix paused. "She does."

"Everything OK?" Luke asked. He could sense that something was bothering her.

"Yeah, nothing I want you worrying about right now," she said.

Luke knew what that meant, and he was troubled by it too. Luke had always been fond of Aurelia, but he and Beatrix had grown closer to each other after three years. What world would Aurelia be coming back to?

He turned toward Beatrix and put his arm around her. He wanted her to relax into his arm, and soon she went to sleep.

The world had changed without Aurelia in it, and Luke had too. He knew he would always be there for Beatrix, and he hoped she could trust that he would. Luke couldn't let her down. Not the way he had let Aurelia down by not going with her on the mission.

He wanted to make sure nothing ever happened to Beatrix. He couldn't bear to lose her. He laid his head back, trying to get the last semblance of rest he'd have for a while.

Chapter 17: Vallis Ossa (Valley of Bones)

The dawning light brightened the tunnel, and they made their way out into the open world. Breathing in the fresh air, they headed northeast toward Vallis Ossa.

Xaine had a few of his guards stationed near a patch of trees by the river that led back to the port. They had horses and supplies waiting for them. Beatrix commanded that one of the soldiers turn back to inform the others where they were headed and rendezvous with them.

They set off toward their destination, moving quickly through whatever cover they could find until it was only the open road that led them there. The horses were pushed to their limits as they carried them farther away from the port.

"How did they know where to meet us?" Marius asked Xaine.

"It's one of the perks of being an Evocator and a secret I'll keep to myself." Xaine smiled.

"Heh. They aren't real guards then," Marius laughed. "I may be old, but I've been around a long enough to know what they are."

Xaine didn't reply.

"I can still smell the tunnels. I doubt I'll ever get these clothes clean enough to wash that smell out,"

Beatrix groaned.

"We're going to have to burn the clothes," Luke said.

Beatrix grabbed a chunk of her white hair and smelled it. Disgusted, she said, "Not going to burn my hair, so the smell better wash out."

"I don't have that problem." Luke rubbed his hand through his short, trimmed hair.

Beatrix swung her arm at Luke and missed. "Not funny."

The sun made its way down to scorching midday, and their horses began to slow their pace. They could see the mountains that towered over Vallis Ossa ahead of them.

"How far into the vallis do we need to go?" Marius asked Xaine.

Xaine pointed toward the ruins of Rubrum Castellum that sat atop the mountains. "See the ruins? It's right below them in an alcove on the other side of the mountains. We'll be there soon."

"There is no cave. My soldiers have checked all along the vallis and never reported anything like a cave," Marius responded.

Xaine smiled and spoke sarcastically. "How detailed are your soldiers? I would know, since I used to be one of them. They traveled the whole length of Vallis Ossa and never reported a cave? I wonder how they would fail to report something significant like that."

"Heh," Marius guffawed.

Luke understood that any soldier sent to report the findings of missing soldiers and Aurelia would wind up not detailing everything in their report. It would end up with meaningless details that meant nothing. Their final reports were nothing out of the ordinary, nothing new, and no sign of Aurelia or the missing soldiers.

Xaine continued. "I had to find a way to hide out for years. Wasn't about to leave an open cave out there for anyone to find."

Luke wondered how Xaine had hidden the fact that he was an Evocator in training for years without anyone finding out, and since they had time on their hands, he decided to ask. "Xaine, how long did you train under Rufus?"

Everyone wanted to hear about that. The others all turned their heads to Xaine, waiting for his response. Guess it had been on everyone's mind.

"Well, first off, not all Evocators are bad," Xaine said, looking around at everyone. "It wasn't easy. Any time I had off from legion training, I was hitting the books hard, then offering myself for the night shift in order to train outside the walls with Rufus and the others."

"There were others?" Luke asked.

"Yeah, about three to four of us at a given time,

though I know there were more," Xaine replied. "It was amazing when I was able to bring my first Inmortuae forth. Scared me half to death, but I knew that it was there awaiting my orders."

Marius glared at him. "Heh. That's why you always took the night shift. I'm trying to remember the names of other soldiers that requested those."

"Don't hurt yourself," Xaine said. "Anyway, I trained with him for two years, give or take. Really, most of it was from the grimoires he gave us, but we got the chance to ask him questions and learn firsthand."

"Why become an Evocator?" Luke asked.

"Come on, it's obvious." Xaine looked to Marius. "Was I a good solider? And be honest."

Marius didn't hesitate. "No."

"See, I was never cut out to be a legionnaire like the rest of you, wasn't built for that sort of thing," Xaine said. "Then we were at war, and there wasn't time to train anymore. Rufus had lost his mind and started opening gateways for the Daemons, and...well, you know the rest."

Luke wanted to know about the other Evocators who trained with Xaine outside the walls. Xaine told him that a few of them left to join Rufus while the others remained where they were, soldiers in the legion. One of the Evocators was the one they had encountered back at port. At first, Xaine mistook it for one of the other apprentices he had trained with long ago, but he could feel the raw power and knew it had to be Rufus. As for the others, they could still be alive or in hiding or could have died in the war. He didn't know.

The mountains started to loom larger as they grew closer to their destination. Luke found a moment to break away and speak with Beatrix alone.

"Beatrix, I've been thinking about all the past dangers we've faced in the last couple of days," he told her. "The soldiers should be at Rubrum Castellum by now, and we should have them escort you back to Arcem Regni."

Beatrix was taken aback for a moment. "You're expecting me to abandon the mission when we are so close?"

"You aren't abandoning it. We're going to get the staff and be right behind you. I don't know what else could happen during that time, and I've already put you in harm's way enough."

"It was my choice to be here," Beatrix told him. "But why now?"

"I don't want anything to happen to you. Back in that tunnel when you fell asleep, it was all I could think about. I failed to protect Aurelia, and I don't want to lose you too."

"What makes you think that you're going to lose me?"

Luke hesitated to reply. Often, he had told people the same thing, and they eventually stopped believing it. He hoped that Beatrix wouldn't treat the feeling like the rest. "My gut."

"Well…" Beatrix began and waited for a moment before continuing. Luke waited for the response that followed most times when he told people he could feel it in his gut. His mother used to tell him to follow his gut like his father did, and she had supported him whenever he felt something. Beatrix continued, "I am not going to back out now, and if your gut is telling you that you'll lose me, there isn't a better place for me to be than by your side."

Now that was unexpected, and Luke had no way out now. If he fought for her to return to the soldiers, he could lose her that way. If she stayed with him, something could happen to her. He felt stuck. "Nice way out of that one."

"Keeping you on your toes," Beatrix said with a smile. "We're at the homestretch. We'll get the staff, meet up with the soldiers at Rubrum Castellum, and be home before you know it."

Luke had to worry. Rufus only needed one of them alive; he had made that abundantly clear to them, but if he sent Beatrix alone now, he could be sending her to her death. Beatrix was going to remain on the mission, and he'd protect her with his life if he had to.

"We're almost there!" Xaine yelled for them to catch up.

Beatrix turned to Luke, "Make sure you keep me in your sight at all times."

"I will," he responded.

They joined up with the others as they began their descent into Vallis Ossa. The rock face was a dull gray, towering above them and leading to the rising cliffs that held the ruins. Bones littered the ground where they walked, of Ancilians, Forsvar, and Daemon alike. The horses slid whenever they crushed the bones beneath them, and they all dismounted in fear that they would fall underneath the weight of the horses.

They slowly descended the slope, rounded the cliff face, leaving their horses behind, climbed up the fallen rocks, and stopped where two rock faces formed an alcove.

"It's right here," Xaine said.

Marius grumbled something under his breath about it only being an alcove, and the others climbed in for a closer look. It looked like any other rock face.

"Give me a minute." Xaine closed his eyes. Blue fire filled his hands, bones rattled together, and the rock face fell inward, revealing a cave. "Follow me." Xaine lifted his hands, the flames burning brighter, filling the tunnel that opened into a large, cavernous area.

Trickles of water could be heard falling along the stones. Xaine's light illuminated the stalagmites hanging from the ceiling, and blue mineral rocks were embedded in the cavernous walls. The ground was covered with hordes of treasure from around the realm. Farther down in the cave sat a staff made of bone. Each piece of the staff was a piece of a vertebra from an unknown creature, held together one by one to form the length of the staff.

Xaine lit torch pedestals to give light to the wondrous sight around them and then raised his hands. "Behold my home away from home." Rats and other creatures scattered about the cavern, avoiding the light.

"This is where you hid out for years?" Beatrix asked as she dropped a piece of armor she had picked up from the stash.

Xaine walked over to stand beside the staff. "Yes. Over the years, I've collected and stored a bunch of things I might need in case of another war."

"Is that his staff?" Luke asked.

"Yes." Xaine waved his hands, and the staff shimmered. "With this staff, I will command one of the greatest armies in the realm."

Luke looked around and saw weapons, shields,

armor, sacks of grain, and piles of gold. "Is that what this is all for? An army?"

Xaine gripped the staff in his hands. The cave entrance slammed shut, and skeletons formed around the room, each lifting a sword into its hands. Blue orbs of fire glowed in their eye sockets, and they stared intently, soullessly, at Marius, Beatrix, Luke, and the last soldier in their column. Xaine's eyes burned with blue as he said, "I already have an army."

That's when the torches went out.

Chapter 18: The Staff of Rufus

Luke's eyes adjusted right away. He had always been able to see in the dark but could only make out distinct outlines. Details were a lot harder to spot. He quickly moved over to Beatrix's shadow and tapped her shoulder. "It's me. We need to form up with the others." He grabbed her hand and led her over to Marius. "Marius, it's us." Luke grabbed his arm before he was clobbered. "We need to create a tight circle and try to go back the way we came."

"Where is Beatrix?" Marius whispered.

"With me. Grab the soldier next to you and follow my lead." Luke began to walk back toward the front of the cave entrance, even though the door was shut.

They stumbled over the horde of treasure on the ground and tried to keep their distance from the blue orbs walking their way.

"Valor," Xaine called out to him. "Where are you going?"

The ground beneath the cave started to shake; something was underneath them.

"They are getting closer," Marius snarled. "Going to have to break a few bones if we're going to make it out alive."

Marius swung his shield at the blue orbs next to him.

He missed, and the eyes rolled further in the darkness.

"Valor! Get behind the Inmortuae!" Xaine yelled, his eyes glowing in the distance. "Stop!"

Hands began to clap behind them, starting off softly and then growing louder and louder with each clap.

"Magnificent," a voice said from behind them, one Luke had heard enough times to fully recognize who it was. "Never thought that the day would come where one of my apprentices would surpass me in strength. Well done. Very well done."

"I don't have time for your games, Rufus. This ends now," Xaine said, and the Inmortuae in his command moved toward the entrance.

Luke began to move the group back toward the floating eyes in the cavern. He decided to take his chances with Xaine instead of Rufus. That's how much of a pickle they were all in.

"We're going with Xaine on this one?" Marius asked as Luke pushed the group toward the floating blue in front of them.

"Be ready for anything," Luke told him and shoved them past the first two sets of floating blue. They weren't attacked. "So far, so good."

Luke had been trying to keep calm during the whole situation, but he could feel the shaky anxiousness of the others. Marius was about to burst from the group and start swinging if Luke didn't maintain his grasp on him. His heart raced; they were trapped in the darkness of this cave with only his limited night vision to guide them through.

"Hang in there—I got you," Luke told Beatrix, squeezing her arm as they moved toward the side of the cave away from the conflict.

The ground shook again, and something moved through the floor beneath them.

Marius stopped, and they bumped into each other. "Why are you stopping?" Luke asked. Marius shushed them.

"Listen. Do you hear that?" Marius asked. "It can't be."

"What is it?!" Beatrix asked breathlessly.

"It can't be," Marius said. Fear was evident in his voice. Luke never knew Marius to fear anything, and that made him worry. "It can't. They haven't been seen in ages."

"Enough fooling around!" Rufus said. The fire illuminated the evil grin on his face as he summoned his own band of Inmortuae.

Chaos followed.

The movement underneath them rushed toward Xaine. Shadows of rocks flew past him, the ground falling inward, while large, shadowed hands emerged near the blue light illuminating off Xaine, and a giant with horns stepped out of the earth.

"A lurker." Marius stared at the Daemon emerging from the ground by Xaine.

Xaine could only be seen moving with the fire in his hands in the darkness, and he began fighting the lurker while the sounds of fighting and bones rattling arose at the entrance.

"I can't tell who we're fighting," the soldier beside Luke said.

"Neither can I," Marius said. "Heh. Guess we're going to just start smashing skulls together."

"Is there no other way out?" Beatrix asked.

Luke could see the wall outline behind them and every shadow fighting within the cave. He tried to keep his eye on Rufus, who was moving toward Xaine at a hurried pace. "Stay against the wall. Rufus is going for the staff. I have to stop him." He let go of the others and stepped away from the group.

Beatrix grabbed his arm, pulling him back, and then loosened her grip. "Was going to tell you to stop, but I know better. Please come back to me."

"I will." Luke found her hand and squeezed it. "I promise." He dropped her hand and moved into the crowd of shadows.

He brought his ancilia out and stepped over the

horde of items along the floor, avoiding any blue-eyed shadows he didn't have to come in contact with. Rufus stepped through them, occasionally dismantling the bones of those who got in his way, his eyes focused solely on the man holding his staff, who was fighting the giant lurker.

Xaine had to keep placing the staff in front of him to knock the clawed hands aside, maneuvering backward before he was pummeled to death. Skeletons rose and engaged the lurker only to meet their end moments later. He was barely holding the lurker back, using some kind of unseen power, but Luke knew that he was using energy to stop the lurker's attacks.

The distance between Rufus and Luke was closing fast. Ducking down, Luke waited for Rufus to make another step. Then he brought his ancile forward in an uppercut. Bones flew upward, blocking the blow from connecting with Rufus's rib cage. Then a fist made of bone smashed into the right side of Luke's face, dropping him to the ground.

Luke felt the fist slam into his back. Instead of falling to his face, he rolled onto his back, lifting the ancilia to protect himself.

Rufus stood above him, fist raised with a gauntlet of bones. "Stay down." Bones scattered along the floor and enclosed his body against the ground, holding him in place as Rufus stepped past him, continuing toward

Xaine.

Moving made the bones poke him uncomfortably. His body, hands, and feet were locked against the ground in a cage of bones. He could see the blue orbs moving toward him, and no matter how hard he shook, he couldn't break free. Steps continued toward him until the orbs stood above him. A skeleton lifted its sword and plunged it downward.

Luke closed his eyes and heard bones shatter. This was it. His life was over. Then he saw a different shadow above him. The skeleton was gone from sight.

The shadow kicked the bones surrounding Luke's body. "Let's go," Marius said, reaching his hand down and pulling Luke up. "I may be blind, but there was just enough light around Rufus to see you go down."

"Thanks. We need to help Xaine," Luke said, looking at Rufus moving in behind the lurker's shadow.

Luke and Marius started forward, moving toward Xaine. Xaine had managed to turn things around and brought the lurker to its knees, then knocked it back with power erupting from the earth below. It fell backward toward Luke.

It landed on its back, and its red eyes flared wide when it saw Luke gazing down at it. Luke didn't wait; he brought his ancilia across its face. The ancilia scrapped into the hide of the lurker, and it turned away from his strike, scrambling back to its hind legs. It now stood before them.

Luke turned his ancilia, extending the length of his blades, which allowed him to keep his distance. The lurker swung its fist toward him, claws extended. Luke brought his weapon down toward the fist. The blade bounced off it, and Luke was lifted off the ground and knocked aside. He could feel the armor pushing in against his ribs, and he fought to catch his breath. Everything looked bright in his eyes, and he could see the lurker's red eyes moving toward him.

Marius roared, and the lurker screamed for the first time in the cave. The shadow of Marius before the lurker could be seen with his shield held high. With the ancile blade being withdrawn from the side of the lurker, its gaze turning toward its new attacker. "That's right," Marius taunted it. He stepped backward, shuffling his feet to avoid tripping. "Follow me."

Luke's breath caught, lungs breathing in air. He gasped, shuffling his hands around to find his fallen ancilia and then took another moment to shake his head, pushing the stars from his vision. He looked across the room and could see the shadows against the far wall, fighting off the skeletons that approached them. His gaze then shifted to Marius; he could see the man moving with an unusual grace to avoid being struck with the fists of the lurker.

With one last deep breath, Luke pushed himself off the ground and rushed the backside of the lurker. With his ancilia extended lengthwise, he slammed against the lurker with all his might. The sound of broken steel echoed throughout the cavern, and the weight of his ancilia became very light in his hands as steel hit the ground in front of him.

"Valor!" Marius yelled.

The lurker turned, and with one clawed hand, it reached for Luke. Stunned he hadn't prepared for a counterattack, Luke saw the claw too late. He fell backward as the Daemon's index finger plunged into his chest. As he continued to fall, the claw left his body. Luke had felt pain before, but his chest burned where the claw had pierced his armor and skin. The muscle ached; then, for a moment, he could clearly see the pain leaving his body. All at once, it pulsed back to the forefront of his mind.

Luke was on his back, watching the red eyes and clawed fist falling toward his chest. Marius roared, and the fist dropped onto Luke's chest, detached from the lurker's body. The lurker reeled back in pain and moved away, back to where it had emerged from the ground.

Marius knelt beside Luke, dropping his shield. He shoved the fist off Luke and lifted him off the ground. "Slow and steady breaths."

Luke's chest burned, but he knew it wasn't fatal. "Help...Xaine," he said between breaths. "I'll be OK."

"Heh. Stubborn to the end, just like your father." Marius ripped a piece of clothing, cut it, and shoved it into his chest wound. Then he pulled him up to a sitting position, lifted his shield, and moved toward the battle raging on between Rufus and Xaine.

Luke gazed upon the battle, breathing slowly, holding the cloth close to his wound, feeling each pulse. Xaine and Rufus had formed an armor of bone around their bodies and were hacking away at each other. Marius wasn't going to make it. He was too far away.

Xaine spun the staff, slamming into Rufus, breaking away chunks of his armor. Rufus allowed the blow and gripped the staff with both hands. Then he pulled it free of Xaine's hands, and the staff split apart, spinning around Rufus's body. The pieces flew and knocked Xaine backward to the ground. Rufus lifted his hand high into the sky. A spear of bone manifested and flew into Xaine, whose arms were outstretched, holding a wall of bone before him. But it wasn't enough.

They had been too late. Marius growled, rushing toward Rufus, and lifted his shield in time to block the pieces of the staff flying toward him. Defending himself, he retreated backward.

Beatrix screamed. Luke looked toward her. The lurker was upon her and the soldier. He tried to push himself upward, feeling the fatigue. "No," he said weakly. "No." He slowly got to his feet.

Light drifted into the room as the doorway fell outward at the cave entrance. The giant shadow of the lurker began rushing toward the cave entrance with Beatrix screaming and wriggling in its remaining hand. The lurker slammed through the rock face, leaving a huge gaping hole in the wall. Light illuminated the cave from the outside.

Marius charged toward her and fought valiantly through the skeletons before him. Rufus had gained control of all the skeletons in the room, and they rushed Marius as Rufus made his exit through the entrance of the cave.

"Beatrix!" Luke screamed. The conflict continued. Marius fought the skeleton horde. Rufus turned at the cave entrance, and Luke could see the evil grin flashing across his face.

"Bring it down," Rufus said, and the skeleton horde turned from Marius and caused the cave's entrance to collapse in on itself.

Luke could see Beatrix staring at him from the arms of the lurker. The rocks continued to fall around the entrance as he staggered toward it. He knew he had to save her. The pain continued to press in on his ribs along with the pulsing in his chest, and he collapsed.

Chapter 19: Trapped

Luke opened his eyes to the surroundings of the cavern around him, bones mingled with the horde of treasure stashed throughout the cavernous floor. Marius sat alone, hunched forward, shield in hand. Xaine was on his back, a spear lodged in his chest, and his breathing was slow. The last Ancilian soldier to protect Beatrix with his life lay still on the stone floor.

For the first time, Luke's vision wasn't the same. Not only could he see the outlines of the shadows; he could see everything clearly in the darkness. It was as though sunlight had flooded into the room and made everything clear before him.

Luke adjusted himself to sit upright. Sharp pains erupted through his body, reminding him of the injuries he had sustained. He moved toward Marius, pushing through the pain, and called out, "Marius."

Marius looked around, knowing where the sound had come from, but his eyes didn't focus directly on Luke. "Can't see anything after shattering the last of the bones. Where are you?"

"On your left." Luke reached his hand out.

Marius reached blindly in the darkness, moving his hand up and down until he found Luke's. "I searched for you in the rubble, kept fumbling my away around, then decided to rest a bit. How did you find me in all this?"

Luke didn't really know himself. "Is it really that dark? Everything looks pale but normal to me."

"Heh. You best be thanking your mom for those eyes," Marius said. "Because you didn't get those eyes from your father."

"My mother?"

"Yeah, her being Forsvar, you must have inherited it from her."

Luke knew that his mother was Forsvar, but inheriting their talents was another thing. He wished he knew more about the Forsvar, the gifts they had, and how they had come to be. Questions filled his mind, and as much as he wanted answers, there was no time. Beatrix was in trouble, and they needed to get out of the cave.

"We need to get out of here and save Beatrix," Luke told Marius. "There has to be a way out."

"You're on your own on this one." Marius settled back, holding his shield. "Nothing I can do in this situation."

Frustrated, Luke moved toward the entrance and pushed the rocks covering the only known exit. Regardless of the pain in his chest and ribs, the stones felt lighter in his hands, and he chucked them easily aside. Another gift from his mother?

The way Beatrix looked at him when the rocks began to fall, closing them off from each other, fueled his desire to clear the way. He was letting her down, breaking his promise that he'd always keep an eye on her. What had he been thinking? That it was all going to work out, that nothing could possibly go wrong? The thoughts became a roar within his mind, and he slammed the rocks to the side, the clumps of dirt and rock shattered against the wall. Sweat began to pour down his face. His arms felt weak; there was no end in sight to the rocks. It was useless to try this alone.

As he laid his back against the fallen rock wall, he thought of leading Marius over to the rocks and instructing him. Easier to just do it himself. He got off the ground and started forward again.

Along with the creaking of rock and the drip of water against stone, he could hear shallow breathing across the room. He had forgotten about Xaine in his rush to get out of the cave. He rushed past Marius and approached Xaine.

The spear of bone had pinned him to the floor, and he was barely holding on. Sunken eyes and shallow breath showed that there wasn't much time left.

"Xaine...I'm sorry." Luke didn't know what else to say. He felt helpless.

Xaine looked around and focused on where the voice had come from. His hand moved to the floor, looking for the voice.

Luke grabbed his hand. "There has to be something I can do."

Xaine turned his hand around until it fell into the palm of Luke's hand. Then he began to spell words.

"Slow down and start over," Luke told him.

Xaine rolled his eyes. He began spelling words with a pause between each word.

"*Ursus. Infected.*"

"Yes, I know that he was infected, but how?"

"*Phys...*" It was becoming hard to figure out the letters he was spelling. Finally, Luke relented to telling him that he could see in the dark and there was no need to try to spell as if they were both blind.

"*Physician.*" He finished spelling the word.

"His physician is the one who infected him? Why?"

"*Evocators*," Xaine spelled with his fingers.

Then it made sense. Rufus had trained the Evocators, and infecting Lord Ursus must have been part of the larger plan.

"*Torch*," Xaine spelled to him.

Torch? Luke thought for a second, trying to connect the dots back to Lord Ursus; then he realized what Xaine meant and looked for a torch around the room.

He picked up a bone, tightly wrapped cloth around the top of it, and brought it back over to him.

"Here," Luke said, bringing the torch closer to Xaine's fallen hand. "It's right here."

Xaine gripped the torch. He then moved his hand to the cloth wrapped about the top and lit it on fire. It burned, and Luke lifted it into the air away from his body. Marius saw the light, rubbed his eyes, and then walked over.

"Feels good to see again, and I don't mind the warmth," Marius said. His face changed upon seeing Xaine pinned to the ground by bone. "You don't look so good."

Xaine grinned and began coughing. The spear shook between each cough, which made things worse.

Luke turned and told Marius what Xaine had told him about Ursus being infected by his own physician. They both agreed that they could do nothing about it in their current situation and needed to find a way out.

The cave shook, and they felt their legs giving out to the massive quaking surrounding them. "Looks like Rufus is beginning to pull the fallen city above ground," Luke said as they steadied themselves. "We don't have much time. The entrance will take us hours if not a day to get through."

"Maybe these quakes will help remove most of the

rubble, and we'll be able to squeeze through," Marius said as another quake began. Stalagmites from the ceiling started to fall and crash to the cavernous floor. "Or we'll die."

Luke thought through what Xaine had told them about finding this cave in the first place. Had he stumbled upon the cave from the outside or through another passage? He knelt beside Xaine and asked him, "Is there another way out of here? You said you found this cave. Did you come through there, or was there another way?" Xaine's eyes were rolling back into his head. He was losing consciousness. "Not yet. Xaine, you have to tell us. Is there another way out of here?"

Xaine tried to focus on Luke, but his eyelids began to close rapidly. He struggled to open them and stared into Luke's eyes. "Forgive me...Aurelia." Then his breathing slowed and stopped.

Luke turned away and held the torch high in the cave. With his last breath, Xaine/Felix had wanted forgiveness from the person this mission was for. Three years to find a single clue had led to so much destruction and chaos in the realm, and he was trapped in a cave with no visible way out. A quest to find Lady Aurelia, only to put Beatrix in the hands of Rufus. There was no use trying to hold in the frustration he felt. He roared, then shook the torch around the cave and let his frustration out as the quakes shook the cave once more.

Marius reached up and took the torch from his hands. "You're going to drop that."

Luke tried to calm down, but holding in nearly three years of anguish and pain had been too long. He glared at Marius and then turned back toward the entrance to throw more stones aside.

Luke continued to throw stones, feeling the pain in his chest, and saw the torch move about the cavern, sending shadows across the walls. It felt good to let his aggression out with each stone he threw, but he couldn't shake the pain away. Why hadn't he just let the past be the past? Would this have even happened if he'd just destroyed the cursed blade in the first place? Another stone left his hands, colliding with the wall. Every step they took toward finding Aurelia left more death in their wake—first at the camp, then at Rubrum Castellum, the Port, and here. He had lost everyone, and he felt helpless, tired, and hopeless.

"I know what you're going through." Marius was behind him. The torch flame danced upon the cloth, and Luke turned toward him. "What you're doing to yourself isn't going to save Beatrix or Aurelia, and if you give up now, you'll always have this moment to look back on with regret."

Luke stared into the old man's green, misty eyes. How could Marius know what he was going through, and why would he care about looking back to this moment and regretting it? He regretted even finding the clue to begin with. "It can be one more thing you can tell me to leave in the past."

"I don't want you to leave this moment in the past. You have to find the courage that I never could. The look in your eyes, the way your body slouches forward, I was exactly like you before I gave up," Marius said.

Luke was sick of the speeches, the words that were meant to bring him out of this moment, and he wasn't going to listen to the old man's wisdom any longer. "The great Marius gave up—so what? Everyone does. Leave me alone." He turned, lifted a stone, and let it fall from his hands. There was no reason to even try anymore.

"Not your father," Marius said, and Luke felt himself lowering his defenses. "The day you were born, he wouldn't let it happen again and rushed through the gateway to where you were born right before the Daemons plunged their spikes into your shoulders. No, not Nero. Courage was always with him in any situation, and whenever I look into your eyes, I remember that I didn't do that for my own son. When my wife gave birth to our son, the Daemons plunged their spikes into his shoulders, all because I had given in to defeat."

Luke sat staring at the rubble before him, listening to Marius tell him the story. Was it true that his father had saved him from such a fate? Had Marius lost his own son to the Daemons? "What happened to your son?"

"He is out there, around your age, alive. Though his mother and he rarely have anything to do with me." Marius laughed to himself. "Even seeing her the other night was enough to get my heart racing."

"That was her back at camp?" Luke asked, turning toward Marius.

"Yes, and I'll never stop loving her." Marius smiled. "Your father was able to change the fate for Cassia. He broke the bonds between her and the Daemons at the cost of his own life, but she was free, given back her agency to choose for herself."

Luke was finally getting answers. Marius was speaking his mind, answering all his questions, but why now? "All these years and you never told me—even my own mother never told me. Why now?"

"Seeing that we may not make it out of this cave alive, I'd feel better not letting my guilty consciousness go to the grave with me, and seeing that Cassia won't have the chance to kill me herself, this felt like a good time to tell you."

The quakes had grown more and more frequent throughout their discussion, and stalagmites continued to fall throughout the cave, but the rubble at the entrance remained.

Luke and Marius continued their discussion as they lifted the stones from the entrance together and tossed them aside. Luke wanted to know why they would give birth in the Daemon realm instead of back at home, and Marius replied that it was their way. They had no choice but to give birth there, and the spikes gave the Daemons dominion over the child as it grew.

Marius's wife had been angry that their son had been subjected to such torment that she kept her distance from him. Though they were married, she had vowed to stay away from him for the rest of their miserable lives. Seeing his son had been hard for him, and his wife kept them far apart from each other, hoping that he would live out his life as a Forsvar, one without freedom.

That was why they continued to fight for the freedom of the Forsvar, to destroy the Daemons binding them and give them a new life.

Luke reflected on the image of the rising phoenix from the ashes and now knew what it meant. The symbol they had back at camp had been on Marius's letter. When he asked Marius about it, he confirmed that it was about freeing the Forsvar and giving them back the right to choose for themselves.

It felt good to sit there talking with Marius this way, hearing the old man give him the information he had been seeking most of his life. Though it felt pointless with no sight of them escaping, it did lift the burdens he had carried around all these years.

"One more question," Luke said. "My mother used to tell my father she had been looking for him; what did she mean by that?"

"Heh. Maybe I *should* make sure we're not going to make it out alive before I tell you about that in case Cassia finds out."

Luke lifted a rock in front of him and chucked it aside. "I don't see us making it out of here anytime soon."

"True." Marius hesitated before continuing, "When Nero had the spikes placed into his shoulders, he lost his agency to choose for himself. Every night he endured torture from the Daemon controlling him, and every morning your mother and others would try to figure out where it was happening. That way, when they entered the realm of Daemons, they could fight their way to free him." Marius stopped briefly before continuing. "They were already too late."

One last and final quake rumbled through the cave, and they gripped the walls to steady themselves. It lasted several minutes. Stalagmites fell, the walls began to creak and groan from the strain put upon them, and the sound of water rushed into the cave and toward them, flowing through the crevices along the floor.

When the rumbling stopped, Marius and Luke looked at each other and then over to the area where the water was flowing into the cave. He wanted to ask more about his father, but there were more pressing matters to attend to. "If we make it out of here alive, let's continue this little chat."

"If we make it out alive, Cassia can never know." Marius gave a sad laugh. "Heh. Not sure which way I'd rather die, to be honest."

"My mother isn't that bad," Luke said as they crossed the cavernous room, avoiding the fallen rocks.

"Heh. I don't think we're talking about the same person. If you ever get the chance to see your mother fight, it will make more sense."

"After what we've been through, I hope I never have to fight again." Luke saw his ancilia lying shattered on the ground. He lifted one into his hand; it looked like Aurelia's. "Whatever that thing was, it shattered my blade."

"That's because you're not using your father's blade." Marius smiled and lifted his ancile up to the torchlight. Luke could see that it was made of different materials. "If I'd known we'd run into one of those things, I would have made you bring them along. Guess I wasn't in the right mindset at the time."

"Are you saying that you have one like his?" Luke

kept staring at the ancile in his hand.

"Heh. Not surprised that you never noticed it. Guess your head was always up in the clouds thinking about Aurelia." Marius kept walking toward the entrance of the flowing water. "Grab his, and let's get going. We have the ladies of the realm to save."

Luke was in awe about seeing another blade like his father's. He knew that his mother had one made of the same material, but Marius? Why did Marius have one? He moved across the room and lifted the shield and ancile from his comrade's hands. He saluted his fallen comrade and ran toward Marius.

"After you. I'm old and can't see as well." Marius waved toward the entrance that had formed from the quakes. "And I'd rather have your back than you having mine."

Luke shook his head and decided that he was glad Marius hadn't given up on him when he had given up on himself. He stepped into the water and started walking upward through the flowing stream. He began to steel himself for what lay ahead, hoping for the courage to do the right thing.

Chapter 20: Waterway Under the Ruins

The stone walls were wide enough for one person to walk through, with high eight-foot solid rock with blue translucent minerals embedded into the stonework. It was well rounded and looked to have been formed by individuals rather than naturally. The water pressed against their ankles, and every step was at an incline, moving them upward away from the cavernous cave below as they continued forward, hoping to find an exit.

Luke thought about what they were about to find at the end of the tunnel. Where would it take them? Closer to saving Beatrix and Aurelia or somewhere else? The way the tunnel was curving, he felt that it would bring them out close to the ruins. It was getting hard to concentrate, and his legs burned with each step.

"The way this water is rubbing against my ankles, it's all going to blister," Luke said.

"Heh. A blister would be the least of our concerns. I'm more worried about what we face ahead," Marius said, climbing behind him.

"Right," Luke said. "Beatrix had sent for reinforcements before we headed for Cymatilis. Hopefully there won't be much left over for us to fight."

"I doubt it. If that lurker is still around, those soldiers won't stand a chance. We weren't prepared for one of those," Marius said.

"How so?"

"Our weapons are useless against their hides; only the ones we forged with the Forsvar work. That's why your weapons broke. They aren't the right material to cut through. They'll never get past that lurker without losing legions, and that's pushing it," Marius said. "When we first encountered those in the war, the soldiers we lost—wasn't worth it. That's when the Forsvar began working with your father to craft a new type of weapon, the ancile.

"The issue was the lack of materials. The Forsvar had minimal access to gather the resources, and very few of them were allied to our cause. Eventually, a handful were crafted and given to the strongest in the legion, your father, mother, Lord Ursus, me, and a few others. Whenever we encountered the lurkers, one of us would have to fight alongside the Forsvar and legions to take it down, and one by one, we advanced.

"The Forsvar already had weapons that could cut through the Daemons, but it took time for us to free them from their oppressors, and others wouldn't be caught fighting with us for fear of retribution."

"Why haven't we tried to make more, gather the materials we can?" Luke asked.

"We've tried, but the Daemons started hoarding the materials and keeping it from being taken. Your mother has tried over the years to get her hands on it, but with no luck." Marius continued, "The lesser Daemons don't have the hides like the lurkers, and if we were to encounter a behemoth at this point, we'd all be dead. Our weapons would be useless. Even mine isn't enough; I got lucky with the lurker down there."

"Behemoth?" Luke asked, curious to understand the names Marius was using.

"Behemoths are the ones who place the Forsvar under their command. It was a behemoth that tried to place its spikes into your shoulders but failed."

"Because of my father?"

"Yes. Behemoths aren't allowed to step foot into our realm, unless called upon and a ritual is performed. Lesser Daemons, the hounds do not follow the same laws that the lurkers and behemoths do. The Forsvar are gateways for the behemoths to interact with our world, and they can open gateways, allowing the lesser Daemons and hounds into our world, and then working together, they can bring lurkers through. However, without a crystallum, a behemoth cannot pass through these gateways."

Marius continued to tell Luke that he was concerned that the Forsvar had been working with Rufus on some level to allow a lurker into their world, and what was happening wouldn't end well. The shard that Luke saw in the image with Lady Aurelia most likely was a crystallum, and if Rufus were to get his hands on that, it would allow a Behemoth to pass through, ultimately leading to their deaths and the destruction of the entire realm.

They didn't know what was up ahead, but if they didn't stop Rufus in time, it would be the end of all they knew.

Luke kept thinking after they had concluded speaking. He thought about what had transpired since they left Arcem Regni on this mission of great importance—at least thought it was—but the realm was now in danger of being destroyed because he had set Rufus free.

Would his life have been simpler if he had just forgotten about Aurelia, with only her statue to remind him, and moved on with Beatrix? Even now, the thought of her being in mortal danger was what drove him to take another step. She was in harm's way because he hadn't thought of anyone but himself.

"Marius, let me ask you a question." Luke didn't really want to hear what the old man had to say on the matter but needed to know if he was right.

"Heh."

"Is what I did wrong?"

"Meaning what?"

"I knew that Rufus's shade was trapped within her blade, but I continued anyway, not thinking about the consequences of my actions. Looking back, I should have destroyed it, but it was the only clue we had about Aurelia."

"Do you really want to know what I think?" Marius asked.

"Yes."

"This entire time you've only thought about yourself. I don't even know if you have seen what it's done to Lady Scorpio. You've been ignorant of how she feels in all of this. Does she want the return of her sister? Yes, we all do. The issue was how you went about it, no matter the risk, no matter the cost to your relationships. You constantly went off into your own world looking for Lady Ursus, and to be honest, I would have left your sorry self a long time ago, and that's why I don't know what she sees in you."

Luke wanted to justify his position, but he knew Marius had a point. He felt the weight of his words. Beatrix tried to talk to him about their relationship, but he kept pushing it off. The signs had been there, but he'd been so focused on finding Aurelia that he had lost sight of what he had been going on around him.

"Neither do I," Luke replied. He didn't know what

she saw in him, and now he might never get the chance to tell her how he felt.

There had been no indication that Lady Aurelia was alive, and he had been walking blindly forward, listening to Rufus and his gut. That had to end. Beatrix was his purpose now. He needed to bring her home before they built a statue of her alongside her sister.

Ahead was a stone wall where water continuously flowed through cracks, and around the corner, they found dry ground ahead of them and could hear the roar of a battle raging down the tunnel where light fluttered in, giving them both the hope they needed.

They sprinted for the tunnel's exit and found rocks blocking their way. As they pushed through the stones, they could hear the fighting beyond.

"Horn formation!" Orders were shouted from their officers, and shadows through the holes could be seen forming together.

Rocks tumbled to the ground, and the light of the moon shone on the battlefield in front of them.

The Inmortuae filled the ruins, fighting the Ancilian soldiers. Hounds engaged the soldiers surrounding them, using their strength and speed to dispatch the unsuspecting soldiers.

A roar captured the attention of everyone as the one-handed lurker stepped into the moonlight, its red eyes and horns set on destroying the invaders.

Chapter 21: Os Monstra

Rubrum Castellum was no longer beneath the earth, but it was a city in ruins, with stones fallen inward, collapsed buildings, and columns leaning to begin their own collapse upon the battlefield. Legion armor littered the ground, weapons from fallen soldiers of years prior in a battle fought on these grounds before it fell beneath the earth.

There stood a large domed building between two towers falling in on themselves at the edge of the ruins. The entire city was filled with Os Monstra—Bone Monsters, the Inmortuae skeletons wearing old legion armor, the Daemon hounds, and behind them all, the massive lurker.

Jagged skin hardened with flames covered the skin of the lurker. Ripples through the skin displayed the massive muscles of the creature, and its horns were bent forward, jutting out the side of its head. Its eyes filled with the hue of red, its mouth displayed a variety of sharp teeth, and the bellowing fires of its belly erupted from its mouth, showing its hatred for the soldiers it now faced. As it leaned forward with one hand missing, its massive fingers were tipped with sharp claws.

The Ancilian soldiers had pushed their way into the ruins from the outside, holding the line and engaging the Os Monstra with caution. Hounds dashed forward, crashing through soldiers unprepared to face them in horned formation.

Through the clashing of shields, bones shattering, and growling hounds, Luke spotted people entering the domed building. White hair streaked across his vision, and he could see Beatrix struggling against her captors.

Luke pointed toward the dome to Marius, who saw them before they disappeared entirely into the domed building. "Beatrix needs us. Lead the way, general," Luke told Marius, who nodded back and rushed toward the aid of the Ancilian legions.

Amid the chaos, Marius shined. Officers received their commands, and Luke was given command of twenty soldiers, who formed up quickly to engage in the conflict. His objective was to take the dome. Marius told him to leave the lurker to him and his soldiers, reminding him that only his weapon would be able to pierce its skin.

Luke moved into the field, behind the twenty soldiers who formed up before him, each facing the battle before them.

"Hold the line! Our objective is to rescue Lady Beatrix, who is being held prisoner against her own will inside that dome. What we do today shall always be carried upon the winds in the realm. Don't fear that you'll be forgotten, for your families shall carry your names into eternity. Make your families proud. What we do is and has always been for the realm!"

Luke stepped past his soldiers in the line and held his shield and ancile above him as they began their march. "Every inch we take brings us closer to victory!" He yelled back to the soldiers.

Inmortuae rushed forward and found their end against the shields of the Ancilians, Luke slamming through skeletons along with his soldiers.

He knew that the hounds were going to be the problem, though they were preoccupied with the other soldiers at the moment. Before them were massive lines of skeletons and, last but not least, the lurker.

Step by step, they covered the ground together, sending more of the Inmortuae to their end. Skeletons tried to break through the line, but with the training and discipline of the soldiers, it was nearly impossible to get beyond their defenses.

"Horn formation, hound incoming." Luke heard the growls before they spotted the hound rushing toward them. The soldiers broke down their line and formed up into solid groups of three, flipping their ancile outward to create the horns extended from the shield. Luke rushed toward two soldiers, raising his shield outward, and the soldiers fell in line with him. Their hands flew to the back of the shield, helping embrace the impact of more giant creatures, and their ancile were held to their sides.

The hound barreled into Luke's shield as he was front and center of the conflict, and it brought them back two steps. Another hound had exploded out from the earth, bringing three soldiers down and ripping them apart. Other soldiers engaged, hoping to save those being ravaged by the hound, and were able to strike a few blows against the hound before it dashed away.

The hound before Luke stepped slowly from side to side, looking for an opening beyond the shield. Luke kept his eyes focused before him and instinctively felt like he had seen this hound before; it was very aware of him, and its eyes were not leaving his. Each step set with a heavy breath, they faced each other. Instead of waiting for the hound to make its move, Luke rushed forward. The soldiers felt the shield moving and moved with him. The startled hound fell back on its hind legs. The soldiers brought their weapons down on the hound and nicked it before it got away.

Luke didn't have time to waste playing games with this hound; he had Lady Beatrix to save, and every moment out here was one he felt he couldn't get back. Keeping his focus on the hound, he continued his rush. The soldiers gazed at him but followed their orders. Luke engaged the hound a few more times before it caught on and leaped for the shield. The weight hit the shield full on, and Luke fell back. The soldiers slammed their weapons into the hound. It continued to press past the shield, ignoring the strikes, its eyes and maw focused on Luke. Its head came over the shield and snapped down toward Luke's face, barely missing. Luke's grip on the shield dropped, and the hound and shield fell to the ground. Ignoring the hits from the soldiers, the hound leaped toward Luke. The blade in his right hand closed in the hound's mouth, and its teeth began pressing against the base of the weapon, leaving his lower arm unprotected. The hound's teeth dug in. He had nothing to hit the hound with and pressed the ancile further into its mouth. Claws pressed against his chest plate as he roared through the pain, continuing to press through the jaw. The hound's grip loosened, and it fell to the ground before him. The soldiers gathered themselves together and helped Luke ensure the hound was down.

Luke felt his body shaking from the adrenaline racing through his veins, and he gazed around the rest of the battlefield. The other hound had been brought down by those in his command, and the ground was cleared of Inmortuae.

The roars of the lurker were now ringing through his ears. The conflict had arrived before the dome. Even as skeletons formed against and rose to fight the legionaries, Marius was now facing off against the lurker himself.

Soldiers were down on the ground, their weapons useless against the hide of the lurker, but they did what they could to distract the massive creature. Hounds continued their deadly strikes, rushing into the ruins, catching a soldier standing alone, as it was hard to spot them in the moonlight.

Shaking the pain off as much as he could, Luke commanded his soldiers to aid the others and prepare to face the lurker. They formed back into the line, with two groups of three remaining in horned formation on the sides to protect against an unexpected hound attack.

Marius had done this before. Luke could tell from the way he moved with the lurker and delivered each strike at the right moment. He was taking the hide away from the lurker, and it began to become fearful. It moved to try to escape the battlefield, seeing that it wouldn't last long with its one arm, but unable to escape, it roared and dug in its heels, facing Marius, its hand and claws extended before him.

Luke knew what was about to happen, and he began to sprint toward them. The lurker was going to sacrifice itself to take down Marius. It didn't care at this point.

There was a grace to how the old man moved. The lurker rushed him, its heels kicking up stone and dirt around it, and it manifested into a cloud in the moonlight. Marius started with a defensive posture, then feinted into avoiding the clawed hand and sliced his way through the lurker cleanly, leaving it to fall into the ruined city.

As Marius lifted himself from the battlefield and shook the dirt from his clothing, cheers erupted from the soldiers.

Luke slowed his approach, glad that Marius had been able to come through it unharmed. He gripped the wound on his wrist, which stung from the hound's bite. Luke had felt a tremendous amount of strength when he pressed his weapon through the hound's mouth, a power he felt that he had never really had before the encounter in the cave. Something had happened in that cave.

They had made it. The dome was open; there was nothing in the legions' path now. It would be moments before they rushed in to save Lady Beatrix and stop Rufus. Luke didn't know if he'd find Aurelia there or not, but the time had finally come for them to end the mystery of her disappearance once and for all.

The legions were still engaged with the last of the Inmortuae. Marius still stood near the fallen lurker, and Luke felt his gut hum with danger. Marius had his back to the dome, and Luke saw the hound bounding through the darkness behind him, each step ever so silent. No one else had heard or seen the hound. "Marius!" Luke yelled as he sprinted across the ruins, and Marius lifted his arm, showing that he was OK. Luke waved and pointed behind him. "Hound, behind you!"

The hound's claws extended toward Marius, whose back was exposed. It brought Marius down.

Chapter 22: Ritus

Soldiers rushed the hound and began hacking away at the beast as it dug its claws into Marius's back. Luke arrived in time to bring his blade down, ending the hound's life, and shoved it off Marius's back.

Marius groaned. The armor on his back was ripped to shreds, and he barely managed to keep his eyes open. Luke held Marius in his arms. "Marius, hang in there. Medici are on their way now." He then turned to yell toward the medical soldiers. "Hurry!"

The soldiers were still engaged with the Inmortuae, and more hounds began to appear from the shadows of the ruins and walked out of the dome. Luke knew that whatever Rufus was doing in the dome was summoning more of these creatures into being.

A line was formed to protect Luke and Marius as the Medici started their work. They stripped the armor off Marius's body and began tending to the gashes along his back. Groaning with pain, Marius stayed conscious. "Heh. Take command…and save them," he croaked, referring to Lady Ursus and Scorpio within the dome. They had come this far and couldn't give up now. Marius gripped Luke's hand and placed the weapon he had used to slay the lurker in it. "Go…they need you."

Time was running out; he needed to act now. He

nodded at Marius and let the Medici do their work. "Legionaries, this realm has thrived and survived upon your shoulders. Don't be troubled that this burden once again falls to you. Our ladies of the realm are beyond that threshold. Our deaths hang in the balance, yet while we draw breath, we have the power to sway that balance in our favor!"

Luke turned. The soldiers cheered as they formed up with him. Lifting the shield and the ancile blade that Marius gave him, he marched upon the dome, followed by the soldiers.

The cylindrical building had a central opening in the ceiling, where moonlight flowed in from the night sky above. A coffered concrete dome flowed downward from the central eye in the sky to large granite columns that sat beneath a pediment.

Soldiers filed into the room in a line of four, shields at the ready. Then they began to spread out into the cylindrical chamber. Moonlight found its way in, illuminating the room, reflecting off the floor where rocks had fallen, cracking the once beautiful craftsmanship. The walls were lined with Inmortuae, and Daemons hovered above the ground, the ones they had fought three years ago along the wall.

It was the Volucer. The bulky gargoyles, wings

flapping in the air, focused on the soldiers entering the building with their red-hued eyes.

At the end of the dome stood an orange transparent ripple, where more Daemons made their way through, joining their comrades in the air or on the ground. Rufus stood with his back facing their entrance, his hands filled with orange and blue flames as he concentrated on the gateway before him.

Beside the gateway suspended in a blue sphere was a woman dressed in legion uniform, holding a crystal embedded in her chest. Some of her hair was up in a loose ponytail while the rest flowed down over her face.

To the right of the sphere stood Beatrix, being held by two Volucers, struggling against the Daemons forcing her forward. When she saw Luke, she fought harder to escape their grasp.

Luke's heart raced to see Beatrix alive, along with the form of Aurelia hovering yards before him. There she was after all this time. He had to stay in control.

The soldiers had formed lines within the dome, their shields at the ready, leaving just enough space for Luke to pass between them, to the front of the line. Luke took a deep breath, remembering that he had to maintain order and control of the situation. He made eye contact with the officers of the columns and signed for them to watch the skies: "*Be prepared.*"

"Rufus! Surrender," Luke yelled out to him.

Rufus turned toward Luke, hands waving through the air. Luke could tell that he was still maintaining the ritual as he spoke. "Feels like déjà vu seeing you standing there. I don't have time for your games, though I am glad to see you've made it out alive, only to die here at the end."

Screeching from the Daemons filled the room, and they flew toward the legion. Luke stepped back to fill the gap between the lines, holding his shield above as they dived. Claws raked the shields, and the Inmortuae rushed across the room.

"For the realm!" Luke roared along with the officers, and they rushed forward into the skeleton horde, with the flying Daemons swooping and diving at them.

Soldiers screamed as they were pulled from the line by a diving Volucer and tossed to the skeletons below.

Luke thought about the strength he had felt during the conflict with the hound and put it to use, slamming his shield through the skeletons before him, sending bones scattering. Yards away, he saw the Daemons holding Beatrix howl when the blue sphere touched their skin, and they began to disintegrate. Another Volucer rushed to their aid, gripping Beatrix by the hair and forcing her toward the sphere.

"Help me clear a path to Lady Scorpio!" he called at

the soldiers beside him, and they formed up with him, pushing forward toward Beatrix.

A claw gripped the side of Luke's shoulder, lifting his feet off the ground. Quickly, Luke brought up his blade, removing the creature's clawed hand, and fell to the stone below. Stabilizing himself, he marched forward, remembering to keep an eye on the sky. Other soldiers hadn't been as fortunate and were lost during their march.

Skeletons came and went before their line, and Daemons fell among the soldiers, only to meet their end at the point of the blade.

Beatrix screamed. The Daemons holding her were becoming frustrated as they tried to force her into the sphere. She broke free and was able to slam her fist into the face of a Daemon before its claws dug into her skin, sending another scream throughout the dome.

Rufus became agitated and said something that Luke couldn't hear above the conflict. Their march was stalled by a horde of skeletons and Volucers that engaged them, forcing them to the defensive. The Volucers that held Beatrix lifted her off the ground and tossed her toward the sphere.

Luke's heart flew into his throat. He watched Beatrix flying toward the sphere. Her skin passed through the sphere without harm, and her body followed. She collided with Aurelia, and they both continued through the sphere to the other side, where the crystal dislodged and scattered across the floor.

Rufus's eyes followed the crystal. Luke didn't have time to really clear his thoughts. He placed Marius's ancile into the sheath along his back, took one from the soldier beside him, and, seeing that Beatrix had passed safely through the sphere and Aurelia with her, flew into motion. He left the line and slammed his way forward through the skeletons, prying the claws away as they tried to grip him.

If that crystal was the one he and Marius had discussed, Rufus couldn't get his hands on it. Few more steps, he told himself. He held his shield before him. The skeleton raised its crude bone weapon and jabbed forward past the shield. Luke couldn't stop the blade. He brought his ancile to slam the skeleton, and, twisting aside, the blade ripped through his armor, leaving a gash against his left side as he collided with the skeleton, smashing it to pieces. He fell to his knee.

No time, Luke told himself, feeling the pain rush to his brain. He had to shut it off. As he pushed himself off the ground, he saw Beatrix moving to her feet. Aurelia stirred upon the floor. "Beatrix!" he yelled and slid the ancile from his hand across the floor to her and tossed his shield.

Beatrix caught the shield before it knocked her over, lifted the ancile, and faced the Daemons that had tossed her through the sphere. She looked angry.

Luke saw Rufus bending over toward the crystallum. He lifted Marius's ancile from its sheath and slid across the ground, kicking at Rufus's feet. His foot connected and brought Rufus down, and he dropped the crystal. Rufus turned toward his attacker, and Luke barely had time to lift the shielded front of the blade to block his fist. The bones he had gathered around his hand shattered against the small shield and shoved Luke across the floor. Luke saw the crystal hit the wall near the portal.

Rufus was already rushing toward it. Luke got to his feet and was able to grab Rufus's foot with his free hand, pulling him back. Rufus turned and backhanded Luke, knocking him down. He wriggled away from Luke's grip and reached for the crystal.

Aurelia grabbed the crystal and pulled it away from Rufus right before his hands wrapped around it. She rushed back, only feet away from the gateway that stood open with the crystal in her hand.

Luke saw where she was going. On the floor was the circle she had stood in with the crystal before. He had to stop her.

Rufus screamed, and every skeleton and Daemon turned to Aurelia and rushed at her.

She entered the circle, and the crystal grew bright

blue, causing a sphere to surround her once more. She locked eyes with Luke, who was a couple of yards away. "I'm sorry," she said as the sphere collapsed around her. The skeletons, Daemons, hit the sphere and started to vanish from sight.

Aurelia had defeated scores of creatures in just a moment.

Rufus continued to panic. He lifted his hands before him, and the portal rippled. Daemons flew inward, free to enter the realm once more to engage the soldiers who continued to press forward. Skeletons began to form from the fallen bones, blue fire entering their eyes, and they pushed the attack, only to meet their end once more.

Luke ran past Rufus, who was now engaged with his ritus. His sole focus was upon Aurelia and the crystal. He had seen how Beatrix had gone through the sphere without it destroying her and remembering what Rufus said about someone who held her dear. He took his chances. He shoved his hand into the sphere, watching the crystal make its way toward Aurelia's chest, and he stopped her.

"No!" she yelled, looking up with her dark-green eyes to focus upon Luke. "Don't do it," she said. Luke felt his heart beat faster. He hadn't heard her voice in over three years and had waited so long for her to return. As he gazed upon her face now, he felt the tears streaming down his face. "I have to do this for the realm!" She continued her rant as he pulled the crystal away from her chest.

"Aurelia," Luke said, his body fully enveloped in the sphere. No one could reach them now. "You don't have to do this. We're safe now." She pulled against him, struggling to keep the crystal in her hands. "Let go of it. Everything is going to be OK." He reached back and placed his ancile into its sheath and gripped her hand. "Lady Ursus, it's time for us to bring you home."

"You don't understand," she said, determined to not let the crystal go. "We can't allow him to let her through."

Luke grabbed it from her and she tried to grab it back. He could feel the crystal trying to force its way to his chest. It wasn't only Aurelia trying to hold on to it. The crystal was trying to find its way into whoever held on to it. Luke pushed the crystal away while fighting Aurelia for it and asked her, "Let who through?"

"It has been a long time, Nero." A woman's harsh voice rushed through the gateway. On the other side stood a Daemon more enormous than the lurker they had faced, horns beautifully formed upon her head, curving around to the sides of her face. Her face looked almost human, with clear features. Her eyes were set with orange fire, and her lips curved upward into a smile, showing teeth bared ever so slightly. Luke looked at her. She was shocked. "You aren't Nero, though you remind me of him. What is your name?"

Luke could see the Daemon clearly through the gateway, but she wasn't through it. Hounds sat at her side. A lurker in the background waiting for its turn to rise to the occasion of entering the realm.

Rufus slowly made his way into the portal, escaping the soldiers who had advanced through the room and cleared the last of the Daemons and skeletons.

"Her," Aurelia said to Luke, her hands reaching for the crystal. "Don't let her through."

Luke had his hands full, trying to keep Aurelia off the crystal and using his strength to stop it from entering his chest. "Beatrix," he called to her, and she rushed through the sphere and pulled Aurelia free of it, bringing her to stand behind the soldiers.

"Who are you?" Luke asked the Daemon on the other side.

"Lucia, my dear young hero. Now if you'll kindly give us the crystal, we'll let you leave until we meet again," the Daemon said from the other side of the portal.

"It's over," Luke said and turned his back on the portal, leaving the circle in the ground. He barely had time to throw his arms around the crystal as it started flying from his hands toward the gateway, taking a step back into the circle. The sphere surrounded him again, trying to make its way into his chest.

"I don't think you fully understand the situation you've put yourself into," Rufus said from the other side of the gateway. "The crystal is attuned to this gateway. As long as I hold the ritus, one step out of that circle, and the way will be opened."

Luke knew in his gut that he was trapped. There was no way out of here alive. He turned to face Beatrix and Aurelia, who were trying to force their way through the crowd. "You have to do it for the sake of the realm!" Aurelia yelled at him. Beatrix couldn't fully understand what was happening, but she saw the look in Luke's eyes and began to shake her head.

"No matter what choice you make, we'll be back for the crystallum," Rufus laughed. "This is only a minor setback in our plans, and next time they won't have their fearless leader with them."

Luke turned toward the gateway; he felt his hands slacking against the tugging of the crystallum. There was no other choice to make now. Aurelia knew the consequences of allowing Lucia through the gateway, and now he had to make a choice for the realm.

He reached back and pulled the ancile carefully out while maintaining his grip on the crystal. He struggled a bit but managed to get it free from its sheath.

"You can't destroy it! I already tried that," Aurelia yelled, seeing what Luke was about to do.

That was how her ancile broke. She had tried to destroy the crystal, then made the ultimate sacrifice for the realm, giving her life. She had tried a moment ago to do it again. That was before Luke had asked Beatrix to remove her from the sphere. Was he willing to do the same? If he couldn't destroy the crystallum, then could he give his life until they figured out a way to save him from the same fate that had befallen Aurelia?

"That look in your eye, the determination not to break under pressure. It was the look that Nero had every time I punished him. There was no breaking that man, and I see it now with you." Lucia spoke from beyond and gasped, "That fire within you, oh my. Are you their offspring?"

Luke stared at Lucia. Was she the one who had punished his father, tortured him every night leading up to his death? "You tortured my father?"

"Then you are his child." She laughed. "Why yes, when I plunged those spikes into him, he screamed in pain, and every night leading up to his death, I made him suffer. Now the venatrix searches for me, but she'll never be strong enough to take me—none of you are."

Luke felt himself stepping forward, wanting a chance to throw down with Lucia. If it opened the gateway, then so be it. Aurelia was safe now, and they could end this once and for all. They would take down every single one of those Daemons as they passed through the gateway.

"Hold the line, and prepare yourselves!" He started forward, seeing Lucia grin, Rufus smiling, and the lurker behind them, all eager to pass through.

Then it hit him. He stopped and stepped back into the circle. The hide of the lurker. There was only one weapon that could cut through that skin. It would be a slaughter. Everyone would die if Lucia could only be struck with the ancile he held in his hands. They didn't stand a chance.

There was only one blade in the entire room that had the power to do what they needed, and it wouldn't be enough.

"Stand down!" Luke yelled. He gazed over and saw Beatrix staring at him, her shield lowered. He gazed at her and mouthed the words, "I'm sorry."

It was over. Luke's chance for Lucia and Rufus would have to be taken up by others. Without the weapons, it was useless. He had to do this for the realm.

Luke turned toward the gateway. "Rufus, you'll have to come and take this crystal yourself. There will always be someone like Lady Aurelia or myself standing in your way, and when we meet again, I'll wipe that grin off your face myself!"

Lucia screamed, and winged Daemons flew through the gateway toward Lady Aurelia. Rufus stopped smiling, and skeletons emerged off the ground.

"For the realm!" Luke yelled. He shoved the crystal to the end of the blue sphere and let it go. It rushed toward his chest, and he hoped that the weapon he had in his hand was enough to destroy the crystallum. His arm was swinging downward with all his might, and screams erupted from beyond the portal. Luke felt two arms wrap around him inside the sphere as white light shattered the realm.

Epilogus

The white light vanished; it fell into the ocean, surrounding the realm from each corner. The screams died away, and the arms around Luke's chest disappeared.

Luke blinked rapidly, passing the light that had blinded him as the crystallum was shattered beneath the blade. His hand was still held forward, and now there was no blade in his hands. Standing upright, he found himself on the wall of Arcem Regni overlooking the fields beyond, where packs of Daemons had formed together and were heading toward the walls.

Marius was speaking in front of him. Officers and soldiers stood at attention, listening. "We will each take a group of Ancilian soldiers and fortify the quarters of this wall. Under no circumstances are we to let a Daemon set foot past these walls, lest you find yourself dead and unable to swing your bloody weapon. Valor, you'll take the first section of the wall; Scorpio has the next section. Amata, you've got this section, and I'll take the last section. Questions?" No questions were raised. "Valor, a moment. The rest of you are dismissed."

Luke watched as the officers departed to their assigned areas. Beatrix Scorpio approached Luke, her white hair layered from the back to the front to allow no hair to fall in front of her eyes. She stopped in front of him. Her ancile blades stood above her shoulders with sharply curved iron in their sheaths.

"Hope it was worth it," she said, fierce blue eyes focused intently on his light-brown eyes. Then she threw her arms around him, hugging him tight, then stepped back. "I don't know why I did that."

Luke stared at her blankly. "What's going on?"

She laughed and then pushed past him. "Felt easier when you were out of the way. Don't do it again."

"What does that mean?" he called after her, but she never looked back.

Marius was staring at Luke as he turned around; he had gray hair cropped short on the sides with short hair on top, in true legion fashion. "Anything I need to know about you and Officer Scorpio?"

"Marius! You're alive!" Luke rushed toward him and tried to hug Marius.

Marius grabbed his arms, "Of course I'm alive— what has gotten into you? First you leave your post, then I find you and Scorpio hugging. Are you feeling all right?"

"Yes, we did it. We found Lady Aurelia, and…" Luke felt a sense of déjà vu. This didn't feel right anymore. Marius looked wide-eyed at him as though he had no idea what Luke was talking about. He had just destroyed the crystallum, and then he was here.

"Heh," Marius said. "Guess you found Lady Aurelia and lost your train of thought. Get to your post and fall in."

"No, Marius. What's going on?" Luke panicked.

"We're at war, and you've to cover the first section of this wall." Marius waved his hand. "Now report to your officers and get your head out of the clouds."

Luke's brain caught up to what was going on: he was back to the moment before Lady Aurelia's last mission, and they would be holding this wall all night. He didn't have time to waste. "Marius, I'm leaving. Lady Aurelia is in trouble, and I have to go help her. My officers can hold the wall without me, and I'm going to need you to lend me two columns to go after her."

Marius stopped, turned slowly, and went up to Luke's face. "My ears may not have heard what you just told your commanding officer."

"Marius, I've done this before. I don't know what is happening, and there is no time to explain. I'm going after Lady Aurelia now, and I'm not going to let you stop me."

"Soldiers, apprehend him," Marius called to the soldiers around him. "Confine him until we get to the bottom of this."

"Marius, you have to believe me. Aurelia is in

trouble!" Luke yelled, stepping back from the soldiers, who looked confused about what was happening. There wasn't time to be stuck under house arrest; the war would end, and they would be back to where they started. "Marius, you have to believe me. Do you remember what you told me about your son?"

"My son!" Marius yelled and slammed his fist into Luke's stomach. "I don't have a son."

The soldiers threw their arms under his armpits, and Luke caught his breath. "I've been through this before. The war ends, and Aurelia never comes back. When we set out to find her, you tell me about your wife and son and the Forsvar, about my father, and how you wished you had the courage that he did. I'm asking you to believe me. Don't make me regret it, the way you regret what happened to your son."

Marius was angry, but before he struck again, he paused. Marius knew he had never talked about his son and shared those details with Luke. "Let him go and return to your posts." The soldiers let Luke go and backed off, even more confused about the situation. "I don't know how you know any of that, but there is something telling me to believe you, and I can't shake it."

Luke walked toward Marius and placed a hand on his shoulder. "There will be plenty of time for me to fill you in when I get back."

"Heh. I'm crazy to even believe a word you're saying. Go before I change my mind. I'll have the soldiers meet you at the main gates." Marius waved him off, walking back toward the wall, grumbling to himself.

Luke rushed away from the wall and headed toward the forge within the central courtyard. It was a long run to make, but it felt worth it. There was something he needed to get back at home before he set out after Aurelia. He had been given a second chance. The whole realm had another opportunity. Whatever had happened, the course of time had changed, and now he could change things.

He opened the door to his house, and someone called after him.

It was Beatrix. "You're going to think I'm losing my mind, but hear me out." She told him that she had started to remember things. About him being in a sphere. It was all foggy, but she had begun to remember everything.

Luke told her that he had remembered as well, and that he was going after Aurelia. Beatrix left her post and told her officers it was about life and death for her sister, and they didn't question her. If there was a chance for her to save her sister, then she'd take it up with her father and mother later.

"We've been given a second chance. There is something I need before we go." Luke shoved open the door and went directly to the cabinet that held his father's armor and ancile blades.

Throwing open the doors, he gazed upon the armor and weapons with a newfound admiration for them. His father had left these for him. Although he had never before wanted to touch or wear them, now was time for him to put on his father's armor and wield his ancilia.